Jack Higgins liv
Leaving school
the Royal Horse Guards, serving on the East German border during the Cold War. His subsequent employment included occupations as diverse as circus roustabout, truck driver, clerk and, after taking an honours degree in sociology and social psychology, teacher and university lecturer.

The Eagle Has Landed turned him into an international bestselling author, and his novels have since sold over 250 million copies and have been translated into fifty-five languages. Many have also been made into successful films. His recent bestselling novels include *The Keys of Hell*, *Day of Reckoning*, *Edge of Danger*, *Midnight Runner* and *Bad Company*.

In 1995 Jack Higgins was awarded an honorary doctorate by Leeds Metropolitan University. He is a fellow of the Royal Society of Arts and an expert scuba diver and marksman. He lives on Jersey in the Channel Islands.

Also by Jack Higgins

The Valhalla Exchange
To Catch a King
Dillinger
The Run to Morning
The Eagle Has Landed
A Prayer for the Dying
The Last Place God Made
Storm Warning
Day of Judgement
Solo
Luciano's Luck
Touch the Devil
Exocet
Confessional
Night of the Fox
A Season in Hell
Memoirs of a Dance-Hall Romeo
Cold Harbour
The Eagle Has Flown
Eye of the Storm
Thunder Point
On Dangerous Ground
Sheba
Angel of Death
Drink With the Devil
Year of the Tiger
The President's Daughter
Flight of Eagles
The White House Connection
Day of Reckoning
Edge of Danger
Midnight Runner
The Keys of Hell
Bad Company

PAY THE DEVIL

JACK HIGGINS

HarperCollins*Publishers*

This novel is entirely a work of fiction.
The names, characters and incidents portrayed in it are the work of the author's imagination. Any resemblance to actual persons, living or dead, events or localities is entirely coincidental.

HarperCollins*Publishers*
77–85 Fulham Palace Road,
Hammersmith, London W6 8JB

www.harpercollins.co.uk

Special overseas edition 1999
This paperback edition 2000
1

Published simultaneously in hardback by
HarperCollins*Publishers*

First published in the USA by
Berkely Books 1999

ISBN 978 0 00 788408 7

Typeset in Sabon by
Palimpsest Book Production Limited
Polmont, Stirlingshire

Printed and bound in Great Britain by
Clays Ltd, St Ives plc

Publisher's Note

PAY THE DEVIL was first published in the UK only by Barrie & Rockcliffe Ltd in 1962 under the authorship of Harry Patterson. The book went out of print very shortly after its first publication, was never reprinted and never appeared in paperback.

The author was, in fact, the writer familiar to modern readers as Jack Higgins. Harry Patterson was one of the names he used during his early writing days.

In 1999, it seemed to the author and his publishers that it was a pity to leave such a good story languishing on his shelves. So Jack Higgins has created an entirely new framework to the original book, added some scenes and made some changes throughout. We are delighted to be able to bring back PAY THE DEVIL for the pleasure of the vast majority of us all who never had a chance to read the original edition.

Take care, for after raising him, it becomes necessary to pay the Devil his due.

Irish saying

Appomattox Station

1865

Prologue

They were hanging a man on the bridge below as Clay Fitzgerald rode through the trees on the hill. It was raining heavily, dripping from his felt campaign hat, soaking into the caped shoulders of his shabby grey military greatcoat.

The man who followed him was black, of middle years, tall and thin with aquiline features that hinted at mixed blood. Like Clay, he wore a felt hat and a frieze coat crossed by a bandolier of shotgun shells.

'We got a problem, General?'

'I'd say so, Josh. Let me have that spyglass of yours, and I wish you wouldn't call me general. I only had one hundred and twenty-three men left in the brigade when General Lee gave me the appointment. Now it's more like twenty.'

Behind them a young horseman eased out of the trees wearing a long cavalry coat in oilskin, Fitzgerald's galloper, Corporal Tyree.

'Trouble, General?'

'Could be. Stay close.'

Clay Fitzgerald took the spyglass then produced a silver box from a pocket, selected a black cheroot and lit it with a lucifer match. He dismounted and walked to the edge of the trees. Black eyes brooded in a tanned face, the skin stretched tightly over prominent cheekbones, one of them disfigured by a sabre scar. It was a hard face, the face of a man few would care to offend, and there was a quality of calm about him, of complete self-possession, that was disturbing.

Eight men on horseback advanced on the bridge below, hooves drumming on the wooden planks. At that stage in the war, it was difficult to distinguish which uniforms they wore, and it was the same with the two prisoners dragged behind, ropes around their necks.

As Clay watched, there was laughter and then a rope was thrown over a bridge support beam, a rider urged his horse away and one of the prisoners went up kicking. There was more laughter, flat in the rain. Clay Fitzgerald swung into the saddle.

He said to Tyree, 'Find the men and fast.' Tyree turned his horse and was away.

Josh said, 'Are you going to be foolish again?'

'I've never been good at standing by, you know that. Wait here.'

Josh said, 'With the general's permission, I'd like to point out that when your daddy made me your body servant, you was eight years old. I've whipped your backside more than once, but only when you needed it, and I've gone through four years of stinking war with you.'

'So what are you trying to say? That you always got your own way?'

'Of course, so let's do it,' and Josh put his heels to his horse.

They went down fast, pulled in and cantered onto the bridge. The eight men, milling around the remaining prisoner, laughing and shouting, settled down and turned. They were all bearded and of a rough turn and armed to the teeth, the uniforms so worn that it was difficult to determine whether they were blue or grey.

The prisoner on the end of a rope was very young and wore a shabby Confederate uniform. He was soaked to the skin, blue with cold and despairing, shaking with fear.

Clay and Joshua reined in. Clay sat there, the cheroot in his teeth; Josh kept slightly back, his right hand in the capacious pocket of his frieze coat. The man who urged his horse toward them wore a long riding coat over whatever uniform. His face was hard, empty of any emotion, black-bearded. He reined up and took in Clay's rank insignia on his collar.

'Well, now, boys, what have we got here? A Reb cavalry colonel.'

'Hey, he could be worth money,' one of the men said.

It was quiet, the rain rushing down. Clay said, 'Who am I dealing with?'

'Name's Harker; and who might you be?'

It was Josh who answered. 'This here is Brigadier General Clay Fitzgerald, so you mind your manners.'

'And you mind your mouth, nigger,' Harker told him. He turned back to Clay. 'So what do you want, General?'

'The boy here,' Clay said. 'Just give me the boy.'

Harker laughed out loud. 'The boy? Sure. My pleasure.'

He snatched the rope holding the young prisoner from one of the men, urged his horse forward and reined in, kicking the boy over the edge of the bridge. The rope tightened.

He turned. 'How do you like that, General?'

Clay pulled out his sabre and sliced the rope left-handed. His right came up from under the cavalry greatcoat, holding a Dragoon Colt. He shot Harker between the eyes, turned his horse and shot the rifleman behind him. Josh pulled a sawn-off shotgun from the pocket of the frieze coat, shot one man on his left in the face, then as fire was returned, ducked low in the saddle and fired again beneath his mount's neck. At the same moment, there was a chorus of rebel yells, and Tyree and a scattering of horsemen came down the hill.

The four men left on the bridge turned to gallop away, and a volley of shots emptied their saddles. The riders milled around, one of them, a small man with sergeant's stripes on a battered grey uniform.

'General?'

'Good man, Jackson.' Clay pulled his mount in at the edge of the bridge and looked down. The boy was on his hands and knees on a sandbank, wrists still tied. 'Send someone down to retrieve him.'

Jackson wheeled away to give the order and Josh, who was talking to the cavalrymen, came over.

'Don't do that to me again, General. This war is over.'

'You sure about that?'

'General Lee's been pushing toward Appomattox Station looking for supplies and relief, only our boys have found there's nothing there: Lee's got twenty thousand men left. Grant's got sixty. It's over, General.'

'And where's Lee now?'

'Place called Turk's Crossing. He's overnighting there.'

Clay looked over the rail of the bridge, where three of his men had reached the boy. 'Good,' he said. 'Then let's go and find him.'

When he and his men slipped through the Yankee lines, it was raining heavily. Turk's Crossing was a poor sort of place. General Lee was billeted in a small farmhouse, but had preferred the barn. The doors stood open and someone had lit a fire inside. The staff, and what was left of his men, were camped around in field tents.

When Clay and his men moved in, Tyree had the day's password when the pickets challenged them. It was always a difficult moment. After all, it was Confederate pickets who had killed General Stonewall Jackson after Chancellorsville.

Clay reined in beside the farm and turned to Sergeant Jackson. 'You and the boys find some food. I'll see you later.'

The riders moved away. Josh dismounted and held his bridle and Clay's. 'What now?'

A young aide moved out of the barn. 'General Fitzgerald?'

'That's right.'

'General Lee would be delighted to see you, sir. We thought we'd lost you.'

Josh said, 'I'll hang around, General. You might need me.'

Lee was surprisingly well dressed in an excellent Confederate uniform, and sat at a table his staff had set up by the fire, his hair very white.

Clay Fitzgerald walked in. 'General.'

Lee said, 'Sorry I can't call *you* general any

longer, Clay. Couldn't get your brigade command ratified. We're into the final end of things, so you're back to colonel. Heard you've been in action again.'

'One of those things.'

'Always is, with you.'

At that moment, a young captain came out of the shadows. He wore a grey frock coat over his shoulders, his left arm in a sling, and carried a paper, which he handed to Lee.

'Latest report, General. The army's fading away. Lucky if we've got fifteen thousand left.'

He swayed and almost fell. Lee said, 'Sit down, Brown. The arm, not good?'

'Terrible, General.'

'Well, you're in luck. I have here the only general cavalry officer in the Confederate army, Colonel Clay Fitzgerald, who's also a surgeon.'

Brown turned to Clay. 'Colonel? I had a message for you,' and then he slumped to one knee.

Clay got him to a chair, turned and called, 'Josh – my surgical bag and fast.'

The wound was nasty, obviously a sabre slash. Brown was sweating and in great pain.

'I'd say ten stitches,' Clay said. 'And whiskey, just to clean the wound.'

'Some men might say that's a waste of good liquor,' Lee said.

'Well, it seems to work, General.' Clay turned as Josh came in with the surgical bag. 'Should be some laudanum left in there.'

Lee said, 'So you're still around, Josh. It's a miracle.'

'You, me and Colonel Clay, sir. Lot of water under the bridge.'

He opened the bag and Brown said, 'No laudanum, Colonel.'

'It could put you out if I give you enough, Captain. Kill the pain.'

'No, thanks. I must have my brain working. The general needs me. Whiskey will do fine, Colonel. Let's get on with it.'

Clay glanced at Lee, who nodded. 'A brave boy, and he's entitled to his choice. Just do it, Colonel,' and there was iron in his voice.

'Then with your permission, sir.'

He nodded to Josh, who took the bottle of whiskey that stood on Lee's table, uncorked it and held it to Brown's lips.

'Much as you can take, Captain.'

Brown nodded, swallowed, then swallowed again. He nodded. 'Enough.'

Clay said, 'Thread a needle, Josh.' He bared Brown's arm. 'You'll feel this. Just hang in there.'

He poured raw whiskey over the open wound, and the young captain cried out. Josh passed over the curved needle threaded with silk.

Clay said, 'Stand behind the chair and hold him.'

Josh did as he was told, and as General Lee watched impassively, Clay poured whiskey over his hands, the needle and the thread, held the lips of the wound together and passed the needle through the flesh, and mercifully at that first stroke, Brown cried out again and fainted.

An hour later, after a meal of some sort of beef stew, Clay and Lee sat at the table and enjoyed a whiskey. Outside, the rain poured relentlessly.

'Well, here we are at the last end of the night on the road to nowhere,' Lee said.

Clay nodded. 'General, it's a known fact that President Lincoln offered you command of the Yankee army on the outbreak of hostilities. No one disputes your position as the greatest general of the war.' He helped himself to another whiskey. 'I wonder how different things might have been.'

'Waste of time thinking that way, Clay,' Lee told him. 'My fellow Virginians were going to war. I couldn't desert them. After all, what about you? You're from good Irish American stock, your father and that brother of his. You went to Europe, medical schools in London and Paris. You're a brilliant surgeon, yet you chose my path.'

Clay laughed. 'Yes, but I'm Georgia-born, General, so, like you, I had no choice.'

'You're too much like your father. I was sorry to hear of his death. Three months ago, I believe.'

'Well, everybody knew he'd been operating schooners out of the Bahamas, blockade-running. He took the pitcher to the well too often. He was on one of his own boats when they ran into a Yankee frigate. It went down with all hands.'

Lee nodded gravely 'Your mother died early. I remember her well. Your father, as I recall, was somewhat of a duellist.'

'That's an understatement.'

'And the elder brother, your uncle?'

'On my grandfather's death, he inherited an estate in the west of Ireland. He had a plantation only twenty miles from here. Left it in the hands of a manager.'

'So what happens now?' Lee asked.

'God knows, General. What happens to all of us?'

'It's simple, Clay. I've had contact with Grant. We meet at Appomattox tomorrow to discuss surrender terms.' He brooded. 'Grant and I served in the Mexican Wars together. Ironic it's ended this way.' He shrugged. 'He's a good soldier and an honourable man. I've already made it clear in a communication that I want all of my men who own their own horses to keep them.'

'And he's agreed?'

'Yes.'

There was a moan from Brown lying on the truckle bed in the corner. Josh, who had been sitting on watch, got an arm around him as the young captain sat up. Clay went to him at once.

'How do you feel?'

'Terrible.'

'Come and sit by the fire.'

'I'll get him some coffee,' Josh said, and went out.

Brown slumped into a chair, and Lee asked, 'Are you all right, boy?'

'Fine, sir. Hurts like hell, but there it is.' He turned to Clay. 'My thanks, Colonel.'

'My pleasure.'

'I was hoping to meet you. Your uncle had a house near here. Fairoaks?'

'That's right. He went to Ireland and left a manager in charge.'

'Well, he used to have a house. Burned to the ground by Yankee cavalry. I passed it two days ago. One of the field hands had a letter. Some lawyer from Savannah called, looking for you. Said he'd be at Butler's Tavern for a week. Name of Regan.'

'I know Butler's Tavern. It's about thirty miles from here.'

'The letter said if he couldn't get you there, he'd be in Savannah. You know this man?'

Clay nodded. 'My father was a blockade-runner. Regan managed his affairs.'

'Sorry I don't have the letter, Colonel. We were in a skirmish with Yankee cavalry just after I got it, and it disappeared.'

'That's fine,' Clay said. 'You've told me what I need to know.'

Josh came in with coffee in a tin cup and gave it to Brown. Clay turned to Lee. 'What now, sir?'

'For me, Clay, Appomattox and the final end of our cause. Humiliation, of course, but I see no need for you and your men to endure it. You have family business to attend to. I think I'd prefer it if you and your men simply faded into the night. I should think that in ones and twos you'd have little difficulty in passing through the Yankee lines, especially in such wooded country.'

'Is that your order, General?'

'My suggestion.' Lee held out a hand. 'We ran a good course, my friend. Just go.'

The emotion was hard to bear. Clay shook hands. 'General.' He turned and walked out and Josh followed.

He found his men under the trees, sheltering under two stretched tarpaulins beside a fire. Sergeant Jackson stood up.

'What's happening, General?'

'Not general any longer. Back to colonel, boys. I've seen General Lee. He carries on to Appomattox tomorrow, where he will surrender to General Grant.' There was a stunned silence from the men. 'It's over, boys.'

Young Corporal Tyree said, 'But what are we

going to do, Colonel? All I know is the war. I joined at fourteen.'

'I know, Corporal. General Lee's suggestion is that we slip away in small groups, pass through the Yankee lines and go home.' He turned to Josh. 'The money bag.'

Josh produced a leather purse from the bottom of the surgical bag. 'Here you go, Colonel.'

Clay handed it to Sergeant Jackson. 'One hundred English gold sovereigns. Distribute it equally. It's the best I can do, and don't let's prolong this. It's too painful.'

'Colonel.' Jackson's voice was a whisper as he took the money.

Clay walked away, then turned. 'It's been an honour to serve with you. Now get the hell out of here,' and he turned again and walked away through the rain.

The rain continued like a Biblical deluge. It was as if the end of the world had come, which, in effect, it had, as Lee's army struggled toward Appomattox, and it was late afternoon when Clay and Josh emerged from the trees on the bluff above Butler's Tavern. It was on the other side of the stream below, an old rambling building of stone, single-storeyed and with a shingle roof. Smoke curled out of the great stone chimney at the eastern end.

'Looks quiet enough to me, Colonel,' Josh observed.

'Well, keep your hand on that shotgun just in case,' and Clay urged his horse down the slope.

They splashed across the ford and advanced to the hitching rail, where two mounts stood in the pouring rain, still saddled.

'A poor way to treat good horseflesh,' Josh said.

'Yes, well not ours,' Clay told him and dismounted, handing him his reins. 'Put them in the barn, Josh, then join me inside. Some hot food and a drink wouldn't come amiss. I'll see if Regan is here.'

Josh wheeled away and Clay went up the steps to the porch, opened the door and passed inside.

There was a log fire in a great stone fireplace, a bar with a slate top, bottles on the shelves behind. A young girl stood behind the bar, drying some glasses. She was no more than eighteen, her straggling hair tied up, and she wore an old gingham frock. Her face was swollen, as if she had been weeping.

Two men sat at a table by the window wolfing down stew from well-filled tin plates. They were both unshaven and wore shabby blue infantry uniforms. They stopped eating as Clay paused, and took in his grey uniform and Dragoon Colt in the black holster. He looked them over as if they weren't there and walked to the bar, spurs clinking.

'Mr Holt, the owner, is he around?'

'Killed three days ago, sir, riding back from town. Someone shot him out of the saddle. I'm his niece, Sybil.'

'Have you anyone to help?'

'Two young black boys worked the stables, sir, but they've run away.'

One of the men at the table sniggered, the other laughed then said, 'Hey, bitch, another bottle of whiskey here.'

Clay turned to face them. 'I figure I'm first in line here. Show some manners.'

One of them, the one with a red kerchief round his neck, started to his feet, and Clay put a hand on the butt of the Dragoon. The man subsided, eyes wild.

Clay said to the girl, 'I was looking for a friend, a Mr Regan?'

'He has a room at the back, sir.'

'Would you be kind enough to tell him Colonel Clay Fitzgerald is here?'

'I'll do that, sir.'

She went through to the back and Clay moved behind the bar, took down a bottle of whiskey and two glasses, as the door opened and Josh entered, water dripping from the brim of his hat.

'Taken care of, Colonel, and I took pity on those two mounts outside, put 'em in the barn, too.'

The two men stopped eating and the one with the red kerchief at his neck said, 'Niggers stand outside in the rain, that's their proper place, and I don't take kindly to you touching my horse, boy.'

Clay laid his Dragoon on the bar, and poured two glasses of whiskey. 'Over here, Josh. A young lady's gone for Regan. Somebody shot Holt.'

Josh produced the sawn-off from his left pocket and came forward. He took one of the glasses and savoured the whiskey.

'Now I wonder who would have done a thing like that, Colonel.'

At that moment, young Sybil appeared, Regan behind her, a small, bearded man of middle years, wearing steel-rimmed glasses. He grasped Clay's hand warmly.

'Colonel, a pleasure to see you alive.' He turned to Josh. 'And you, Joshua.'

'You've news for me, I believe,' Clay said. 'You left word at Fairoaks.'

'That's right. Let's sit down.'

He drew Clay to the fire and sat opposite him. Josh leaned against the wall, watching the two men. Sybil stayed behind the bar, drying glasses.

'I had business in the area, Clay, and hoped you'd be close to Lee, and I wanted to check out things at Fairoaks.'

'It's not good, I hear.'

'Burned to the ground by Yankee cavalry. Nothing for you there, Clay.'

'Never thought there would be.'

'The thing is, I've got more bad news. Your uncle Sean died a month ago and left you no money, only two properties: Fairoaks, burned to the ground, and Claremont, the old family house in Ireland that he returned to when your grandfather died. In a manner of speaking, it's suffered a similar fate. It's half burned to the ground.'

'What are you telling me?'

'There's trouble in Ireland these days, lots of

trouble. Rebels who call themselves Fenians, who want to throw the English out.'

'But my uncle was Irish American.'

'Who owned a big house, a large estate. The aristocracy's seen to be on the side of the establishment.'

'Hell, at the end of it, what does it matter?' Clay told him. 'Two burned-out properties. I end up with nothing.'

'Not really,' Regan said. 'I've got documents with me for you to sign, relating to your uncle's estate. Then I need you in Savannah.'

'And why would that be?'

'To appear before Judge Archie Dean for your identity to be accepted by the court at the request of the Bank of England in London.'

There was a pause. 'Why?' Clay persisted.

'Your father made a fortune blockade-running, Clay, but he was always foxy and he knew the South would lose. So, he deposited his funds in London and some in Paris.'

Clay said, 'What are we talking about?'

'Well, forget about American currency. Confederate money is a joke and the dollar is strained. If we stick with pounds sterling, I'd say there's somewhere over a million.' There was silence as

Clay stared at him, and Regan said lamely, 'Of course, I do have my fees.'

Clay looked up at Josh in astonishment, and behind them, the man in the red kerchief snarled at Sybil, 'Hey, bitch, let's have another bottle.'

She hesitated, then took one down from a shelf and came from behind the bar. As she reached the table, the other man grabbed her, pulled her on his knee and yanked up her skirt. She cried out.

Josh said, 'God, how I hate that.'

Clay stood up, walked forward and produced the Dragoon. He rammed the muzzle into the forehead of the one fondling the girl. 'Let her go now or I'll blow your brains out.'

The man released his grip slowly, Sybil slipped away. Red Kerchief said, 'No offence, Colonel.'

'Oh, but you have offended me,' Clay told him. 'Take their pistols, Josh.' Josh complied and Clay stood back. 'Out we go, straight to the barn, and be sensible. Just ride away.'

They stood glaring at him, then turned and walked out through the door, Clay and Josh following them. Clay stayed on the porch and watched Josh take them to the barn, shotgun ready. They went inside. A few moments later, they emerged on horseback.

'Damn you to hell, Colonel!' Red Kerchief called, and they rode away.

Josh turned and moved back to the porch.

In the darkness beyond the fence, Red Kerchief turned and reached into his saddlebag, taking out a Colt. 'You got your spare?' he demanded.

'I sure as hell do,' his companion said.

'Then let's take them,' and they turned and galloped back out of the darkness, already firing.

Josh turned, dropping to one knee, and gave Red Kerchief both barrels. Clay's Dragoon came up in one smooth motion and he shot the other out of the saddle.

Sybil and Regan came out of the door behind and Clay said, 'No problem, child, we'll dispose of the bodies before we leave.'

Regan said, 'You all right, Clay?'

'Not really,' Clay said. 'I've been killing people for four years. Frankly, I could do with a change.'

Joshua walked back, reloading his shotgun. 'What kind of a change, Colonel?'

Clay holstered his Dragoon, took a cheroot from his silver box and lit it. He blew out smoke. 'Josh,' he said, 'how would you like to go to Ireland?'

Ireland

1865

1

The coach lurched violently to one side as a wheel dipped into a pothole and the luggage piled upon the opposite seat was thrown against the man sleeping in the far corner, hat tilted forward over his eyes.

Clay awakened as the vehicle came to a halt. They had been four hours on this apology for a road, and since leaving Galway conditions had got steadily worse.

He glanced out of the window at the rain soaking into the ground. The road ran through a narrow valley beside a small stream, with a scattering of trees on the far side shrouded in mist. He opened the door and stepped down into the mud.

Joshua said, 'Correct me if I'm wrong, Colonel,

but I always understood you to say that Europe was civilized.'

He wore a heavy greatcoat buttoned tightly to his chin and a horse blanket was draped across his knees. Rain dripped steadily from the brim of his felt hat as he sat with the reins of the coach in his hands.

Clay turned slowly and grinned. 'This is Ireland,' he said. 'My father always told me God made things a little bit different here.'

Joshua wiped rain from his face with one sleeve. 'I'd say the good Lord forgot about this place a long time ago, Colonel. I'm beginning to wonder what we're doing here.'

'So am I, Josh,' Clay told him. 'So am I.' As the rain increased in force with a sudden rush, he continued, 'You look like a drowned rat. Better let me take over for a while and you can ride inside.'

'I'm so wet already, it doesn't make any difference,' Joshua said.

Clay shook his head. 'No arguments. Come down and get inside. That's an order.'

His tone brooked no denial and Joshua sighed, threw back the blanket and started to clamber down. At that moment, two horsemen moved out of the trees and splashed across the stream.

The leader reined in sharply so that his horse danced sideways on its hind legs, crowding Clay against the side of the coach and splashing him with mud. A shock of yellow hair showed beneath the brim of his battered hat, and the eyes above the red bandana which covered the lower half of his face were vivid blue. His rough coat was buttoned up to the neck and he held a shotgun crooked in his left arm.

Four years of being on the losing side in a particularly unpleasant war had taught Clay Fitzgerald to accept the vagaries of life as they came. He produced his purse and said calmly, 'Presumably, this is what you want?'

Before the man could reply, his companion, who had reined in on the other side of the coach, moved round and said in an awed voice, 'Would you look at this now, Dennis? A black man. Did you ever see the like?'

The man addressed as Dennis laughed. 'Every time a Spanish boat puts in at Galway.' He snatched the purse from Clay's hand and hefted it. 'Rather light for a fine gentleman like yourself.'

Clay shrugged. 'Only a fool would carry more in times like these.'

The man slipped the purse into a pocket and

leaned forward. 'That's a fine gold chain you've got there,' he said, pointing to Clay's waistcoat. 'Would there be a watch to go with it?'

'A family heirloom,' Clay told him. 'My father left it to me. You'd get little for it.'

The man reached down and grabbed for the chain, tearing it free with a ripping of cloth. He held it up and examined the watch. 'A gold hunter, no less. I've wanted one all me life.' He shook his head reprovingly. 'You've not been honest with me, me bucko, and that makes me wonder what might be travelling with you in the coach.' He turned to his companion. 'Pull his baggage out into the road and go through it quickly.'

The boy dismounted, pushed Clay roughly out of the way and leaned inside the coach. After a moment, he turned, a black leather bag in one hand. 'You'll find nothing of value in there,' Clay told him. 'Only some surgical instruments and medical drugs.'

The boy opened the bag and examined the contents. 'He's telling the truth, Dennis,' he said, holding it up so that his companion could have a look.

'So you're a doctor, are you?' Dennis said.

Clay nodded. 'Among other things.'

'I've the greatest respect for the profession,' Dennis told him. 'On another occasion, I'd let ye pass, but these are hard times, and at least you'll have the satisfaction of knowing your money is going to a good cause.' He nodded to the boy. 'See what else ye can find.'

Clay thought of the hundred gold sovereigns hidden inside his spare riding boots at the bottom of the leather travelling trunk and sighed. He slid one foot forward tentatively, ready to grab for the shotgun when the right opportunity presented itself.

At that moment, a cry sounded from somewhere nearby, that was immediately followed by the flat report of a rifle, muffled by the rain. The bullet dented the ground beside the coach. Dennis cursed, trying to control his frightened horse with one hand, as he turned and looked behind him.

Several riders were plunging down the hillside toward them, and Dennis turned and menaced Clay with the shotgun. 'Up with you, Marteen,' he said to his companion.

The boy swung a leg over the broad back of his mare and dug his heels into its sides. Without a word, Dennis followed him. They splashed across the stream and broke into a canter on the other side, disappearing like shadows into the mist.

Joshua scrambled down to the ground and leaned against the coach while he mopped his damp face with a handkerchief. 'Colonel, what kind of a country *is* this?'

Clay shrugged. 'Everything that lawyer told me in Galway must be true. I thought he was exaggerating.' He grinned. 'Don't tell me an old campaigner like you was frightened?'

'I stopped being frightened after Pittsburgh Landing, when we rode into that Yankee artillery regiment in the dark and you bluffed our way right out again,' Joshua told him. 'I was only worried in case you tried something silly.'

'I must admit I was thinking about it,' Clay said.

Joshua snorted. 'Then that shot came just in time to save you from getting your fool head blown off.'

At that moment, the riders who had been making their way down the hillside reached the coach. Three of them galloped straight across the stream without stopping and disappeared into the mist on the other side. The fourth reined in his horse and dismounted.

He was in his early thirties, thick-set and muscular, in muddy jackboots and tweed riding coat, his mouth cruel in a pale face. Clay disliked him on sight.

The man glanced curiously at Joshua and touched the brim of his hat briefly with his riding crop. 'Colonel Fitzgerald?' Clay nodded and he went on, 'It seems we arrived not a moment too soon. My name is Burke. I'm Sir George Hamilton's agent. He heard you had arrived in Galway yesterday and sent me to meet you. Did you receive his letter safely?'

Clay nodded. 'It was waiting for me when I visited my uncle's lawyers yesterday.' He smiled ruefully. 'A pity you didn't arrive five minutes sooner. I'd have been fifteen sovereigns and a gold watch the richer. Have you any idea who they were?'

Burke shrugged. 'The country is swarming with such rogues. If we catch them, they'll tell the judge they were true patriots collecting funds for the organization and damn the Queen's eyes in the same breath.'

'I see,' said Clay. 'Do these men belong to this Fenian Brotherhood I heard so much about in Galway?'

'Fenians, Moonlighters, Ribbonmen.' Burke shrugged. 'There are several of these secret societies, all hell-bent on setting Ireland free, as they call it.' The rain continued its steady monotonous downpour and he went on briskly, 'But this is no place for a conversation, Colonel. Sir George is hoping you'll spend the night with him. If you'll get back in to your coach, I'll lead the way.'

Clay shook his head. 'That's very kind of him, but I prefer to go on to Claremont tonight. Is it far from here?'

'Drumore is another four miles along the road,' Burke told him. 'Claremont is about a mile the other side of it.' He seemed to hesitate, a slight frown on his face and then went on, 'You'll find cold comfort there tonight, Colonel, and that's a fact. The house isn't fit for man nor beast.'

'But I understand my uncle was living in it until his death,' Clay said. 'Surely it can't have deteriorated to such an extent?'

'But you're forgetting about the fire,' Burke said.

Clay shook his head. 'No, the lawyers gave me full details. I understand the damage was extensive.'

Burke nodded. 'Most of the house went. Your

uncle lived in the west wing for the last six months of his life. It was the only part left with a roof.'

Clay shrugged. 'There have been many occasions during the past four years, Mr Burke, when I desired nothing more of life than a roof over my head – any kind of roof. If my uncle managed to continue living there, I'm sure I'll survive.'

'Suit yourself, Colonel.' Burke swung into the saddle of his horse and gathered the reins in his left hand. 'One thing more,' he said. 'Mind how you go when you reach Drumore. They don't take kindly to strangers.'

'Not even to one called Fitzgerald?' Clay asked, with a smile.

Burke's face was grim. 'These are hard times, Colonel, as I think you'll be finding out for yourself before very long.' He spurred his horse forward and disappeared around a bend in the road.

Clay stood gazing after him, a frown on his face. He turned and said to Joshua, 'What do you think?'

Joshua shrugged. 'It can't be any worse than some of the places we slept in during the war, Colonel. One thing's for sure, I don't like that man.'

Clay grinned. 'As usual, we're in complete agreement. There's something unpleasant about him, something I can't quite put a finger on, but it's there.'

Thunder rumbled faintly in the distance and he reached into the coach and, taking out a heavy overcoat, pulled it on. 'It looks as if the weather intends to get worse before it gets better, and I'm beginning to get bored with this particular view of the countryside. If you'll get in, we'll move on.'

For a moment, Joshua hesitated, as if he intended to argue the point, and then he sighed heavily and climbed inside. Clay slammed the door behind him and then pulled himself up into the driver's seat and reached for the reins. A moment later, they were moving along the muddy road.

Rain dripped from the edge of his hat, but he ignored it, his hands steady on the reins. He considered his conversation with Burke and asked himself again, and not for the first time, why he had come to Ireland.

Certainly there had been nothing to keep him in Georgia. Four years of war had left him with only one desire – peace. It was ironic that he should have come to Ireland of all places in search of it. If the stories he had been told in Galway were true, and the events of the past hour seemed to bear them out, he was stepping straight into the heart of an area racked by every conceivable kind of outrage and murder.

The elementary justice of Ireland's claim to self-government was something he had learned at his father's knee, together with harsh, bitter accounts of the treatment meted out to the unfortunate peasantry by English landlords. Later, his years as a medical student in London and Paris, and then the war, had all conspired to push the matter into a back corner of his mind as something relatively unimportant, in that it did not affect him personally.

However much the native Irish had right on their side, highway robbery was no way in which to attract sympathizers, he reflected, thinking of the two thieves. It occurred to him for the first time that although their clothing had been rough, their horses had been superb animals and he frowned, wondering who they were and what had driven them to such a deed.

Perhaps they were members of this Fenian Brotherhood he had heard so much about? He brushed rain from his face and dismissed the thought from his mind. Whatever happened, he intended to keep strictly neutral. At most, he would stay at Claremont a month or two. After that, Sir George Hamilton could have his way and buy the place at the price suggested in the letter Clay had found waiting for him in Galway on the previous day.

It was dusk as they came into Drumore and rain was still falling steadily. The cottages were small and mean, with roofs of turf and thatch, and the blue smoke from their fires hung heavily in the rain. There were perhaps twenty or thirty of these dwellings scattered on either side of the narrow, unpaved street for a distance of some hundred yards.

About halfway along the street, they came to a public house, and as Clay heard the sounds of laughter from inside, he reined in the horse and jumped to the ground.

The building was rather more substantial than the others, with a yard to one side and stables in which several horses were standing, their flanks steaming in the damp air. The board nailed to the wall above the door carried the legend COHAN'S BAR in faded lettering.

Joshua leaned out of the window. 'What have we stopped for, Colonel?'

Clay shook rain from his hat and replaced it on his head. 'Remembering Burke's account of the state of things at Claremont, a bottle of brandy might come in very useful before the night is out. Have you any money handy?'

Joshua fumbled inside his left sleeve and finally extracted a leather purse, which he passed across. Clay opened it and took out a sovereign. 'This should be enough to buy the place up, from the looks of it,' he said, giving Joshua his purse back. 'I'll only be a moment.'

The door opened easily at his touch and he stepped inside, closing it behind him. The place was thick with smoke and illuminated by two oil lamps which swung from one of the blackened beams supporting the ceiling. A turf fire smouldered across the room and eight or nine men crowded round the bar, listening attentively to a tall youth of twenty or so, whose handsome and rather effeminate face was topped by a shock of yellow hair.

For the moment, Clay remained unnoticed and he stayed with his back to the door and listened.

'And what happened then, Dennis?' a voice demanded.

Dennis leaned against the bar, face flushed, a glass of whiskey in one hand. 'It's for a good cause, me fine gentleman, says I, and if you're honest with me, you'll come to no harm. His face was the colour of whey and his hand was shaking that much, he dropped his purse in the mud.'

A young boy of fifteen or sixteen was standing beside him and he said excitedly, 'Show them the watch, Dennis. Show them the watch.'

'In good time, Marteen,' Dennis said. He emptied his glass and placed it ostentatiously down on the bar. Someone immediately filled it and Dennis slipped a hand into his pocket and pulled out Clay's hunter.

He held it up by the chain so that it sparkled in the lamplight, and an excited murmur went up from his audience. 'Would you look at the elegance of it,' someone said.

Clay moved forward slowly and stood at the edge of the group. The first person to see him was Marteen and his blue eyes widened in astonishment. Men started to turn and Clay pushed his way through them until he faced Dennis. 'My watch, I think,' he said calmly.

There was a sudden silence. For several moments, Dennis stared stupidly at Clay, and then he seemed to recover his poise. 'And what the hell would ye be meaning by that?'

Clay gazed slowly around the room. The faces were hard and unfriendly; some stupid, others with a glimmering of intelligence. Then he noticed the man who leaned negligently against the wall at the far end of the bar. He was tall and powerful, great shoulders swelling beneath his frieze coat.

His hair was the same colour as Dennis's, but there the resemblance ended. There was nothing weak in this man's face, only strength and intelligence. He picked up his glass and sipped a little whiskey and there was a smile on his lips. He gazed into Clay's eyes and it was as if they knew each other.

Clay turned back to Dennis and said patiently, 'The money isn't important, but the watch was my father's.'

No one moved. Dennis scowled suddenly, as if realizing his reputation was at stake, and thrust the watch back into his pocket. He picked up his shotgun, which was leaning against the bar, and rammed the barrel into Clay's chest. 'I'll give ye five seconds to get out, me bucko,' he said. 'Five seconds and no more.'

Clay gazed steadily into that weak, reckless face, then turned abruptly and walked to the door. As he reached it, Dennis said, 'Would ye look now? He's messed his breeches for the second time this day.' For a moment Clay hesitated, and then as laughter swelled behind him, he opened the door and passed outside.

He pushed Joshua roughly out of the way and dragged a carpet bag out onto the coach step and opened it. He was not angry and yet his hands shook slightly and there was a familiar, hollow sensation in the pit of his stomach.

'What is it, Colonel?' Joshua demanded in alarm.

Clay ignored him. He found what he wanted at the bottom of the bag, his Dragoon Colt, the gun which had been his sidearm ever since his escape from the Illinois State Penitentiary with General Morgan in '63.

He hefted the weapon expertly in his right hand and then walked quickly to the pub door and opened it again. Laughter swelled to the ceiling as Dennis further embellished his story, and for the moment, Clay was again unobserved.

A stone whiskey bottle stood on the bar near

Dennis's elbow some twelve feet away. It was not a difficult shot. Clay levelled his weapon and pulled the trigger. The bottle exploded into pieces like a bomb, showering the men with whiskey and scattering them across the room.

Dennis's face had turned sickly-yellow in the lamplight and his eyes were round and staring. His tongue flickered across dry lips as he frantically looked for assistance. No one moved and there was fear on every face, except for the tall man who still leaned against the wall at the end of the bar, but now his smile had gone and he held his right hand inside his coat.

Clay's face was a smooth mask, inscrutable and yet in some way terrible. He moved forward and touched Dennis gently under the chin with the cold barrel of the Colt. 'My watch!' he said tonelessly.

The youth's face seemed to crumple into pieces and he produced the watch and purse and placed them on the bar top with shaking hands. 'God save us, sir, but it was only a joke,' he said. 'No harm was intended. No harm at all.'

For a moment longer, Clay gazed fixedly at him, and somewhere a voice said in a half-whisper, 'Would ye look at the Devil's face on him.'

Sweat stood on Dennis's brow in great drops and there was utter fear in his eyes. Then Clay turned away, slipping the Colt into his pocket. The youth lurched to a nearby chair and collapsed into it, covering his face with his hands.

The publican, a large red-faced man, faced Clay across the bar and wiped his hands nervously on his soiled apron. 'What's your pleasure, sir?' he asked.

'Presumably you deliver liquor to local residents?' Clay said.

'I do indeed, sir,' the publican assured him. 'I supply Sir George Hamilton himself.' He produced a dirty piece of paper and moistened a stub of pencil with his tongue. 'What would ye like, sir?'

Clay pocketed his watch and purse and gave his order in a calm, flat voice, as if nothing had happened. 'And I'll take a bottle of brandy with me,' he added.

The publican pushed the bottle across and Clay picked it up and started to move away. 'By what name, sir, and where shall I deliver it?' the publican demanded.

For the first time, a smile appeared on Clay's face. 'I was forgetting. Claremont House – Colonel Clay Fitzgerald.'

He turned away as an excited buzz of conversation broke out and, opening the door, went outside.

Joshua was standing by the open door of the coach and an expression of relief appeared on his face. 'I was watching through the window, Colonel,' he said. 'Next to your father, you're the most cold-blooded man I ever did meet.'

Clay handed him the brandy and pushed him back into the coach. 'I've got my watch back, which is more than I anticipated. All I want now is a meal and a fire. Whatever else we find at Claremont House, I hope we'll be able to supply those things between us.'

As he moved to step up to the driver's seat, the door opened behind him and closed again. Clay turned slowly, his hand sliding into his pocket. The tall man was facing him and he held up a hand and smiled. 'No trouble, Colonel. I only came to thank you for not killing my brother.'

Clay took a quick step forward and brushed back the man's unbuttoned coat, revealing the butt of a pistol sticking out of his waistband. 'I noticed where you had your hand,' he said wryly.

The other nodded. 'Sure, and I saw that you'd noticed.'

Clay shrugged. 'He was in no danger. I'm not in the habit of killing boys. A whipping would be more in his line.'

'When his father hears of this day's work, he'll get that and perhaps more,' the big man said. He held out his hand and Clay took it. 'Kevin Rogan, Colonel. I knew your uncle well.'

Clay's eyes widened in surprise. 'Would you be kin to Shaun Rogan – Big Shaun, as I believe they call him?'

Kevin Rogan smiled. 'My father – why do you ask?'

'I met a friend of his in New York,' Clay told him. 'A man called O'Hara – James O'Hara. He gave me a package for him. If Dennis had stolen it, I wonder what your father would have said to that.'

A strange smile appeared on Rogan's face. 'You'll be doubly welcome if you visit us with news of James O'Hara, Colonel. There's a track starts at the back of Claremont House. Follow it three miles over the moor and you'll come to Hidden Valley. Rogan soil, every foot of it bought and paid for.'

'Perhaps tomorrow,' Clay said. 'Tell your father to look for me.'

He pulled himself up into the driver's seat and slapped the weary horse lightly with the reins. It started to move forward into the gathering dusk. As they turned past the tiny church at the end of the street, he glanced over his shoulder. Kevin Rogan waved at him and then opened the door and went back inside.

2

The house loomed unexpectedly out of the night, a dark mass beyond a low wall, and Clay turned the coach in between stone pillars from which the iron gates had long since disappeared.

The drive circled the house and ended in a large, walled courtyard where Clay brought the coach to a halt. It was then that he received his first surprise. Light showed through the mullioned windows, reaching out into the rain and shining upon the wet flagstones.

He jumped down to the ground and Joshua climbed out of the coach and joined him. 'What do you make of it, Colonel?'

Clay shook his head. 'I couldn't say, but we can soon find out.'

The door opened to his touch and he entered into what was obviously the kitchen. Beams supported the low ceiling and logs blazed in the great stone fireplace, casting shadows across the room. Clay went and warmed his hands, a slight frown on his face.

Joshua busied himself with lighting an oil lamp, one of two which stood upon the table. As it filled the room with soft light, he gave a sudden exclamation. 'Look at this, Colonel.'

Clay moved across to the table, as Joshua removed a white linen cloth revealing a loaf of bread, eggs, a side of ham and a pitcher of milk. A small sheet of blue notepaper carried the words WELCOME TO CLAREMONT in neat, angular handwriting.

Clay studied the message for a moment. 'No name,' Joshua said, stating the obvious. 'Now wouldn't you call that a strange thing?'

Clay raised the sheet of notepaper to his nostrils and inhaled the fragrance of lavender. His eyes crinkled at the corners. 'I thought it looked like a woman's writing.'

'But who is she?' Joshua demanded.

Clay shrugged. 'A Good Samaritan. She'll declare herself in her own good time.'

Joshua lit the other lamp and illuminated the

entire room. There were pictures on the wall, a carpet before the fireplace and comfortable chairs. There was an atmosphere of peace over everything, as if the man who lived here had been happy.

'One thing's for sure,' Joshua said. 'That man Burke didn't know what he was talking about.'

Clay nodded. 'I don't think my uncle's last days can have been too unpleasant.'

He took one of the lamps and crossed to a door in the far corner. It opened directly onto a flight of wooden stairs and he went up them quickly, Joshua at his heels carrying the other lamp. He opened the first door he came to and went in.

The room was small, but comfortably furnished as a bedroom, with a carpet on the floor. The mahogany wardrobe was empty and so were the drawers in the tallboy, but the blankets on the bed had recently been aired and the sheets and pillows were clean and white.

For no reason that he could put his finger on, he knew that this had been his uncle's room, and for a moment he stood in silence by the window, staring out into the night, trying to form in his mind a picture of the man he had never seen.

There was a slight cough, and he turned to find Joshua standing in the doorway. 'I've checked the other rooms, Colonel. There are five, all told. The room next door is furnished with a bed made up and ready for use. The others are empty.'

'Then that takes care of both of us,' Clay said. 'Anything else along the corridor?'

Joshua shook his head. 'Just a blank wall at the end.'

Clay led the way back downstairs. 'I should say these were once the servants' quarters. Presumably they were the only rooms fit for use after the fire.'

He crossed the kitchen to a door on the other side and tried to open it. It refused to budge and then he noticed the large key in the lock. He turned it quickly and the door opened without any further trouble. He was standing in a stone-flagged corridor that smelt cold and damp. Somewhere he could hear rain falling and he moved along the corridor, the lamp held out in front of him.

He mounted a short flight of stone steps and opened the door at the head of them. Immediately, he felt rain on his face and hastily placed one hand protectively over the open end of the lamp.

He was standing in what had obviously been the entrance hall of the house. A great stairway lifted into the darkness on his right and before him lay the scattered, dangerous mass of debris that had once been the roof and upper storey.

For a moment, the irony of the situation struck him. That seven hundred years of his family's turbulent history should come to this and that he, the last of his name and born in an alien land, should stand among the ruins of a great house. A sudden gust of wind caused his lamp to flicker wildly and he turned back down the steps, closing the door behind him.

As he went back into the kitchen, Joshua came in from the courtyard, a bag in each hand. He placed them carefully on the floor and straightened. 'I think you ought to have a look in the stables, Colonel,' he said. 'You'll find something mighty interesting there.'

Clay followed him out into the courtyard. The stables lay on the other side, their great doors standing open to the night, and he saw that Joshua had taken the coach and horse into shelter. A lantern hung from a nail and Joshua lifted it down. 'Over here, Colonel.'

There was a soft whinny from the darkness, and when Joshua raised the lantern, Clay saw a horse standing in one of the stalls. It was a beautiful animal, a black mare with a coat like satin. A thrill of conscious pleasure went through him as he gently ran his hand across its hindquarters.

'Another gift from our Good Samaritan?' Joshua said.

Clay smiled. 'She can make this kind of gift any time she wants. That's one of the finest bits of horseflesh I've ever seen.'

'Things get more surprising round here minute by minute,' Joshua said.

He replaced the lantern on its nail and started to unhitch the coach horse. Clay moved forward quickly. 'I'll see to that,' he said. 'You get a meal started.'

'As you say, Colonel.' Joshua pulled two more pieces of baggage out of the coach and walked across the courtyard to the house.

Clay took off his coat and unhitched the coach horse. He found an old blanket and gave the weary animal a rubdown. Afterwards, he led it into one of the stalls and gave it some of the oats and hay with which the black mare had been plentifully supplied.

The rain seemed to be slackening a little and he stood in the entrance and gazed out into the courtyard, breathing deeply, savouring the freshness. He was tired and his stomach craved food, but there was still something to be done. He pulled the leather travelling trunk out of the coach, hoisted it onto his broad shoulders and trudged across the courtyard through the rain.

He took the trunk straight up to his room. When he went downstairs again, a smell of cooking filled his nostrils. Joshua was bending over the fire, an iron frying pan in one hand.

'Smells good, whatever it is,' Clay said.

The man smiled cheerfully. 'Ham and eggs and fried bread, Colonel. I'll see what I can rustle up tomorrow when I've got the hang of the stove.'

'We've dined on worse, and often,' Clay said.

The bottle of brandy he had got at Cohan's was standing on the table, which Joshua had made ready for the meal. Clay poured a generous measure into one of the cups and carried it to the fire.

He subsided into a chair with a groan of pleasure, booted legs outstretched. 'Best part of the day, Colonel.' Joshua grinned. 'That's what you always used to say on campaign.'

Clay swallowed some of the brandy. An expression of astonishment appeared on his face and he laughed and drank some more. 'Something wrong, Colonel?' Joshua asked.

Clay shook his head. 'Things grow even more mysterious, that's all. This is some of the finest French brandy I've ever tasted. Now where would a broken-down little country publican like Cohan get such stuff?'

'I wouldn't know, Colonel,' Joshua said, as he ladled hot food onto two plates. 'But one thing's for sure. Ireland is no fit place for a gentleman.'

'And Georgia is, I suppose?' Clay grinned as he took his place at the table. 'I don't think the Irish would appreciate your sentiments. In fact if the crowd in that pub was a fair sample of the locals, I'd keep your observations to yourself if I were you. They reminded me strongly of Hood's Texans.'

Joshua shuddered and sat down in the opposite chair. 'Nobody on earth could resemble Hood's Texans, Colonel, unless the Devil went to work in two places at the same time.'

They ate in silence, each concentrating on the heaped plate in front of him. After a while, Clay sat back with a sigh and reached for the brandy bottle. 'Joshua, I always did say that where food is concerned, you're a miracle worker.'

Joshua took the praise as his just reward. 'True, Colonel, only it was your father who said it first.

That's why he hung on to me when everything else had to go in those bad years before the war, after your mother died. He always said he'd have been lost without me.'

'And so would I,' Clay assured him.

Joshua didn't appear to consider the statement needed any contradiction, and busied himself with clearing the table as Clay went back to his seat by the fire and relaxed.

He sipped his brandy and stared into the flames, more tired than he had been in a long time. Gradually, his eyes closed and his head nodded forward. He took a deep breath, forced himself to his feet and yawned. 'It's been a long day. I think I'll have an early night. There'll be a lot to do tomorrow.'

'I'll bring your coffee at seven,' Joshua told him, and Clay nodded, picked up one of the lamps and opened the door to the staircase.

It was cold in the bedroom. He placed the lamp on the small table beside the bed and opened the window. The rain had stopped and the darkness was perfumed, as a small wind lifted from the trees beyond the courtyard. He breathed deeply, inhaling the fragrance of the wet earth. Then the tiredness hit him again and he had barely sufficient strength to strip the clothes from his body and climb into bed. He blew out the lamp and the darkness moved in at once to welcome him.

Clay was not aware of coming awake, only of the fact that he was lying there and that moonlight drifted in through the window with opaque, white fingers.

For a little while he lay staring up at the ceiling, wondering what had caused him to awaken, and surprised to find that he no longer felt tired. He reached to the small table beside his bed and picked up the gold hunter. It was almost two o'clock, which meant that he had slept for no more than five hours. As he watched, the moonlight faded. He threw back the bedclothes and padded across the floor to the window.

It was a night to thank God for, the whole earth fresh after the rain. He stood there, his skin crawling with excitement, a small, restless wind touching his naked flesh. It was a quiet night, the only sound a dog barking several fields away. Then the bank of cloud rolled away from the moon and the countryside was bathed in a hard, white light. The sky was incredibly beautiful, with stars strung away to the horizon where the hills lifted uneasily to meet them.

At that moment, he became aware of another sound, a hollow drumming that was somehow familiar. As he leaned out of the window, a rider, etched against the sky, appeared from the trees beyond the courtyard and galloped along the rim of the valley where the moors began.

As he watched, the rider reined in his mount sharply so that it reared up on its hind legs. For a brief moment, the horse and rider were like a statue, completely immobile. Clay stared up toward them and suddenly, for no reason he could analyse, knew he was being watched. As he drew back quickly, a gay mocking laugh drifted down toward him and the horse snorted and leapt forward, as if the spurs had been applied, and disappeared over the rim of the valley.

Clay dressed hurriedly, his brain clear and cool. There had been too many mysteries already at Claremont; this was one he intended to solve. He went downstairs silently, boots in one hand, and paused in the kitchen to put them on. A moment later, he was crossing the courtyard to the stables.

He opened the door, allowing the moonlight to

stream inside, and as he moved toward the black mare through the darkness, she whinnied softly as if she had been expecting him. He found a saddle and bridle hanging by the stall. They were of English make and lighter than he was used to, but he quickly led the animal out of her stall and saddled her.

As he tightened the girth, there was the scrape of a shoe behind him and he turned quickly. Joshua was standing there, reproach large upon his face. 'Damn your eyes for an old night-owl,' Clay told him.

Joshua sighed. 'What you do nights is your own affair, Colonel, but going by what's happened already, you'd be doing me a favour if you took this.' He held out a belt from which was suspended the Dragoon Colt in its black leather holster.

Clay took it from him and buckled it about his waist. 'Anything for peace. I swear you're more fussy than an old woman.' He swung up into the saddle. 'Now go back to bed – that's an order.' He clicked his tongue and the mare moved out of the stable door and across the courtyard before Joshua could reply.

When he reached the rim of the valley, he paused

and looked about him. The dog still barked hollowly in the distance, the sound somehow bringing back to him so many hot summer nights in Georgia, when, as a boy, he was unable to sleep and had longed to do just this.

He urged the mare into a canter, and as they came out onto a stretch of springy turf, broke into a gallop. It was an exhilarating experience as he crouched low over her neck, the wind cold on his face. They must have covered a good mile when he started to rein in and halted beside a clump of trees.

He leaned down and gently rubbed the mare's ears. 'You beauty!' he said softly. 'You little beauty!' And the mare tossed her head and rolled her eyes as if understanding what he said and liking it.

A horse whinnied from somewhere nearby, and as the mare replied, he hastily turned into the trees and dismounted. Several horsemen appeared over a small rise no more than twenty or thirty yards away. They paused and he heard one of them say quite clearly, 'It was a horse, I tell you, and not far from here.'

Clay placed a hand over the mare's muzzle and waited. One of the men laughed. 'You're jumpy tonight, Patrick, and that's the truth of it. What's there to be worrying about, with Burke and his men waiting at the north end of the estate for poachers who'll never turn up?'

They moved forward and a string of pack animals followed them from behind the rise. Clay waited until they had disappeared over the skyline a quarter of a mile away before following them.

As he topped the rise, a strong wind started to blow in his face and he ran his tongue over his lips, tasting the salt and knowing that he must be very near to the sea. The string of horses had disappeared and he paused and examined the landscape.

The moor itself was clearly exposed in the bright moonlight, but a narrow valley cut through it, dark with shadow, and he realized that this was the route they had taken. He started to move forward again and reined in sharply as a stone rattled somewhere behind him. He turned in the saddle, but there was no one there.

He waited for a little while, but nothing moved and he shrugged and took the mare down the slope, her hoofbeats silent on the turf, and entered the valley.

A well-defined path lay clearly before him and

he urged his mount into a canter, eyes probing the darkness ahead. Ten minutes later, the track started to drop steeply and he stopped. Somewhere below, the sea surged against rocks and he heard voices.

He took the mare straight up the sloping side of the little valley and emerged onto a flat spread of turf that ran gently down to the cliff edge a short distance away. He dismounted and walked forward cautiously.

The bay was crescent-shaped and beautiful in the moonlight. A schooner lay a hundred yards offshore, sails furled, the tracery of her rigging like black lace against the night. He flung himself down on his face and peered over the edge of the cliff. It dropped cleanly to the beach below, the valley path appearing to be the only route down.

The horses were standing at the water's edge and several men were unloading a longboat with a skill which argued a long experience at the task. They appeared to be enjoying themselves, and there was some horseplay as two of them waded through the surf to the boat. A laugh drifted up, clear in the night air.

'At least we now know where Cohan obtains his excellent brandy,' Clay mused softly, and at that moment, the cliff edge started to crumble beneath his weight.

A shower of stones and earth rattled down the face of the cliff to the beach below and the men grouped round the boat turned in the same second and looked up toward him. A piercing whistle cut through the night, and as he scrambled to his feet and turned to run, someone fired a shot, the bullet droning into the night.

Obviously the operation was not being as carelessly conducted as he had imagined, for, as he swung a leg over the mare's back, three horsemen appeared over the rim of the valley and galloped toward him.

He gave the mare her head and she responded well. As they reached the first swell of the moors, he leaned low over her neck, urging her on with coaxing words. He could hear the cries of his pursuers behind him, and the mare hardly faltered as she scrambled up and over the rise.

He was now passing over unfamiliar ground, and as the moors started to lift on either hand, he realized that he had entered a narrow valley. He glanced back over his shoulder. The first horseman was no more than fifty yards behind him and he urged the mare forward, allowing her to pick her own way over the boulder-strewn ground.

A moment later, he cursed and reined in sharply. He had reached a dead end, a blank wall of stone that lifted forty or fifty feet into the night, with a stunted thorn tree growing at the top if it. On either side, the valley slope was as steep as a house roof.

He was not afraid as he heard the first of his pursuers enter the valley, simply annoyed that violence should be forced upon him. He drew the Dragoon Colt, moonlight glinting on its brass frame, and waited as he had waited so many times in the past, with no fear in him now that the moment was at hand.

A gay mocking laugh that was somehow familiar floated down from the clifftop, and he turned in the saddle, arm extended to fire. The rider he had first seen from his bedroom window no more than an hour earlier, had appeared beside the thorn tree.

'Let the mare try the slope if you want to save your skin, Colonel,' a clear voice called. 'She can do it, I promise you.'

Clay didn't hesitate. His pursuers were almost upon him. He fired once into the air to hold them and urged the mare toward the steep side of the valley.

She responded magnificently. He leaned low over her neck, placing his weight forward. A few feet from the rim of the valley, she started to slip on the wet turf. He jumped from her back, grabbed the bridle in one hand and scrambled up, pulling her after him. A moment later, they were over the top.

'This way, Colonel,' the rider called, turning away, and Clay swung into the saddle and galloped after, ignoring the cries of rage which came from below as his pursuers realized that he had eluded them.

The moor stretched before them in the moonlight, sloping gently up toward the hills, and the mare crossed it at a dead run. Clay looked back over his shoulder and saw the three riders appear over a rise several hundred yards in the rear. There was a familiar hollow feeling of excitement in his stomach and he concentrated on overhauling his companion.

The mare covered the ground effortlessly, and slowly the gap narrowed until the two horses were almost abreast. The unknown ally wore an old tweed jacket and broad-brimmed hat pulled low over the eyes. Clay caught a sideways glance and heard a laugh and then they were plunging down into a wide, tree-filled valley following a sandy track.

The rider swerved into the trees and Clay followed, twisting and turning, receiving a thorough soaking as wet branches whipped against him. They emerged into a broad meadow, took a low fence together, landing in a spatter of mud on the other side, and reined in before a ruined stone hunting lodge.

Clay slid to the ground and stood beside the mare, running a hand gently over her heaving side. 'I'm obliged to you, sir,' he said.

The other held up a hand in warning and motioned him to silence. They could hear hoofbeats approaching rapidly as their pursuers followed the track. Within a few moments they passed, and after a while there was silence.

The rider still sat motionless, head forward, listening to the hoofbeats die away into the night, then turned to Clay with a gay laugh. 'The poor fools will run for a mile before it occurs to them that we might not be out in front after all.'

The voice was clear and sweet like a ship's bell across water. Clay frowned and took a step forward. As he did so, his unknown rescuer turned towards him, uncovering with a flourish and allowing a long switch of dark hair tied with ribbon near the crown of the head, to fall freely to shoulder level and beyond.

'Well, I'll be damned,' Clay said softly.

The face that smiled impishly at him in the moonlight was that of a young girl of no more than eighteen years. She was small and slightly built, the man's riding coat too big for her. The eyes were unusually large and set too far apart for conventional beauty, the nose tilted above a wide, generous mouth. There was about her an irresistible appeal, an attraction that was as immediate as it was compelling.

'Who the devil are you?' he demanded. 'Diana the Huntress or the Goddess of the Night?'

She tilted back her head and laughed, the moonlight full upon her young face. 'I had heard that Southern gentlemen were renowned for their chivalry, Colonel, but this exceeds all my expectations.'

Responding to her mood, he removed his hat and bowed gravely. 'Colonel Clay Fitzgerald, at your service. You have the advantage of me, ma'am.'

'Oh, no, Colonel,' she said. 'I much prefer to

remain Diana the Huntress or even the Goddess of the Night for just a little while longer. Women are incurably romantic.'

He started to replace his hat, and as he did so, she touched her mount with the spurs so that it bounded forward across the meadow, cleared the fence with room to spare and plunged into the shadows of the trees. A silvery laugh floated back to him, and as he swung a leg over the mare's back he knew that he was too late.

He reached the track in time to see the girl and her horse briefly silhouetted against the sky as they topped the rise at the head of the valley, and then they were gone.

When he reached the place himself, there was no sign of her. He took a cheroot from his case and lit it carefully, hands cupped against the slight breeze from the sea. He frowned, wondering who she could be, and then a slight smile came to his face. If her performance tonight was anything to go by, she would not leave him long in doubt.

He cantered back toward Claremont, enjoying his cheroot and the stillness of the night. When he reached the ridge above the house, he paused and gazed toward the distant mountains of Connemara. They made a spectacle to take the breath away, and the moonlight silvering the sea filled him with the beauty and wonder of it.

He had made the mistake of coming to Ireland in search of peace, but already he was glad he had come. The thought of tomorrow filled him with a vague, restless excitement, and as he took the mare down toward the house, there was a smile on his face.

3

The morning was grey and a light rain was falling as Clay rode out of the courtyard and followed the track that led up through the trees over the top of the moor.

In one of his old military saddlebags he carried the package he had been asked to deliver to Shaun Rogan, and as he rode, head bowed against the rain, he wondered idly what it might contain.

Of the man who had given it to him, he knew little. He had met O'Hara casually at a party at someone's house in New York, and during the conversation his intended trip to Galway had been mentioned. Later in the evening, the man had asked him to deliver the package and Clay had agreed, thinking he would probably hear no more about it. When he boarded the boat on the following day, it was waiting for him in his cabin, with a polite note thanking him in advance for the favour.

There was already a suspicion at the back of his mind that O'Hara had used him and that the package was something out of the ordinary. From what he had seen of the Rogan family already, there could be little doubt that the contents were of a dubious nature.

He dismissed the subject from his mind for the moment and gazed about him. The mountains were shrouded in mist and visibility was poor, but yet there was a freshness to everything that gladdened the heart, and the air was like new wine. He started to whistle softly between his teeth and urged his mount into a canter as the rain increased in force.

As Kevin Rogan had promised, the track ran for some three miles across the moor and then dipped unexpectedly into a wide valley. Below him in the midst of a clump of old beech trees an ancient, grey stone farmhouse was rooted into the ground.

The place seemed prosperous and in good repair,

with neat, well-kept fences to the large paddock. As he cantered down toward it, a woman moved out of the porch, a pail in each hand. She paused and looked toward him, then she put down the pails and stood with one hand shading her eyes.

She was tall and gaunt, her face wrinkled by a lifetime's care. The hair that showed from beneath the shawl which covered her head was iron grey. She gazed up at him, no expression in her faded blue eyes, and Clay touched the brim of his hat. 'Mrs Rogan?' She nodded and he went on, 'My name's Fitzgerald. Is your husband at home?'

She shook her head, and said in an unfriendly voice, 'He's away for the day.'

'Might I ask when you're expecting him?' Clay said.

She picked up her pails. 'He comes and goes. You'll be wasting your time if you wait.' Without another word, she turned away and walked across the courtyard to a cow byre.

Clay watched her until she had disappeared inside, a slight frown on his face. Then a voice said quietly from behind, 'You mustn't mind my mother. She doesn't take kindly to strangers.'

The man who had spoken stood in the doorway of the stables and cleaned his hands on a rag, eyes calm in a lean, intelligent face topped by the familiar Rogan hair.

Clay walked the mare toward him, and smiled. 'Dennis, Marteen, and Kevin I've met already in that order. Who might you be?'

The other smiled. 'I'm Cathal, Colonel. The quiet one of the family. Kevin said you might drop by sometime today.'

'Your father's not at home, I take it?'

Cathal nodded. 'Pressing business in Galway. He and the boys won't be back until late tonight.'

Clay leaned forward and looked inside the stable door. There were at least thirty horses ranged on both sides in neat stalls, and he whistled softly. 'You've got some good stuff there.'

'We should have, Colonel. We breed them.' Cathal ran a hand over the mare's muzzle in a familiar manner and spoke softly to her. 'But not one of them to match Pegeen, here.'

Clay raised his eyebrows in surprise. 'You know the mare well, then?'

Cathal smiled. 'The joy of your uncle's old age. If there's a better mount between here and Dublin, I've yet to see it. Miss Joanna's taken good care of her.'

Clay resisted the temptation to ask the obvious

question and there was a slight pause. Cathal Rogan made no attempt to continue the conversation, and after a while, Clay smiled. 'Well, I'll be moving on. Tell your father I'll call again tomorrow.'

He wheeled Pegeen away from the stable entrance and Cathal said, 'I understood Kevin to say you had a package for us, Colonel?'

'For your father,' Clay said over his shoulder. 'And I prefer to deliver it personally.' He cantered through the gate and followed the track back up toward the head of the valley.

When he reached the top, he paused and looked down toward the farm. Whatever else they might be, the Rogans were certainly an inhospitable clan and strangers were definitely not welcome – that much both Cathal Rogan and his mother had made plain.

As he started to turn away, there was a movement in the trees beyond the farm. He leaned forward and waited. A moment later, half a dozen horsemen galloped through the beech trees and entered the yard.

The woman came out of the cow byre, carrying her pails, and one of the men swung to the ground and approached her. They stood talking and Clay saw her shake her head vehemently and then the man pushed her so that she staggered back, dropped her pails and fell to the ground, milk spilling across the cobbles.

He wondered what had happened to Cathal Rogan, and in the same moment saw him run from the other side of the stables to the rear of the house. As the woman picked herself up from the ground, he appeared in the doorway, a shotgun in his hand. He raised it to his shoulder and one of the men rode his horse up the front steps, crowding him against the wall and kicked the gun from his grasp.

Clay didn't hesitate. He took Pegeen down the steep grassy slope of the valley toward the farm, ignoring the track and leaning back in the saddle. They reached the bottom safely and Pegeen scrambled up out of the hollow onto the track and galloped past the paddock toward the yard.

One of the riders was still on his horse, but the others had dismounted. Cathal Rogan backed against the wall, as four of them moved in on him while the other started to turn the horses out of the stable. He fought desperately, but within seconds was sliding to the ground under a barrage of flailing fists.

One of the men lifted a heavy boot into his side and Mrs Rogan screamed and ran forward, clawing at his coat. He flung her to the ground with a curse and turned back to Cathal.

Clay arrived at that precise moment. He ran Pegeen in amongst them, scattering them to each side and lifted his boot into the man's face. He screamed once and staggered back against the wall, sliding down to the ground without another cry.

Pegeen danced daintily on her hind legs, swirling to meet the man on horseback who moved toward them with an oath. Clay found himself facing Sir George Hamilton's agent.

Burke's face was dark with passion and his eyes sparked fire. 'By God, Colonel, you go too far,' he cried. 'Stay out of that which doesn't concern you. We're here on Sir George Hamilton's business.'

'I've just decided to make it mine,' Clay told him. 'Does your master usually instruct you to assault old women and generally behave like border ruffians?'

One of the men reached for Cathal Rogan's shotgun, which was lying at the foot of the steps. Clay saw the movement out of the corner of his eye. His hand disappeared inside his coat. When it came out, he was holding the Dragoon. He fired almost in the same movement, the bullet glancing from the cobbles at the man's feet so that he gave a cry of alarm and moved hastily.

Clay's face was expressionless and he held the weapon negligently by his side. 'First, I think we'll have the horses returned to the stables, Mr Burke, and then we'll leave.' He pointed to the man sprawled against the wall, unconscious. 'I fancy I may have broken his jaw. You'll know better in the morning. If I have, send him along to me and we'll see what can be done. You're aware I'm a surgeon?'

Burke glared at him, hate on his face. Clay returned the gaze steadily. After a moment, a shudder seemed to pass through the man's body and he gave the necessary order.

The men quickly rounded up the few horses which had been released and returned them to the stable. Then two of them hoisted their unconscious companion across his horse, tying him into place with a rope they produced from a saddlebag.

Mrs Rogan was kneeling beside Cathal. He pushed her away and struggled to his feet. His face was battered and bruised, but he managed a smile as he looked up. 'We're obliged to you, Colonel. You'll find the Rogans don't forget their friends – or their enemies,' he added, turning to Burke.

'I'll escort these gentlemen from the premises,' Clay told him. 'I think I can promise you they won't be coming back.'

Cathal suddenly looked sick. He swayed slightly and his mother moved forward and supported him with an arm. Together they went up the steps into the house and Clay turned and looked at Burke. Without a word, the agent led the way across the yard, and his men followed.

Clay brought up the rear, still holding the Dragoon ready. They followed the track up onto the moor and halted at the edge of a small wood.

Burke gave his men an order and they moved away. As Clay holstered his gun, the agent said, 'I shan't forget this, Colonel.'

'Neither shall I,' Clay told him simply. For a moment longer, Burke's eyes bored into his, and then he wheeled his mount sharply and galloped after his men.

Clay watched them until they disappeared over a rise a short distance away, and as they did so, a familiar voice said, 'He makes a bad enemy, Colonel Fitzgerald.'

This time she was more conventionally attired in

blue riding habit and tricorn hat, with a small white feather to one side that was limp and bedraggled in the rain.

He smiled and urged Pegeen to meet her as she rode out of the trees. 'I didn't realize the Goddess of the Night rode by day. You know Burke well, then?'

'I should, he's my uncle's agent.' She held out her right hand in an oddly boyish gesture that somehow suited her. 'I'm Joanna Hamilton, Colonel Fitzgerald. Your uncle and I were good friends.'

'That I can believe.' He held her hand lightly in his and she made no attempt to withdraw it. 'It would appear that I have several things to thank you for, Miss Hamilton. A cheerful welcome at the end of a long road and the care of the finest bit of horseflesh it's ever been my fortune to own, not to mention the saving of my fool neck.'

She laughed gaily and shook her head. 'I take no credit for that at least, Colonel. I arrived at the head of the valley some twenty minutes ago in time to see you go into action. On top of that, I understand you caused something of a sensation in Cohan's public house last night. I can now understand why it took the Yankees four years to defeat the South.'

Clay shrugged. 'Don't forget such things are exaggerated in the telling.'

She shook her head. 'My uncle unfortunately takes a rather different view.'

He frowned slightly. 'I'm afraid I don't quite follow you.'

'It's simple,' she said. 'In the first place he's a magistrate. In the second, he doesn't like the Rogans. Burke told him this morning that two of them had been responsible for holding up your coach on the Galway Road yesterday.'

'A boyish prank, over and forgotten,' Clay told her. 'I fail to see how it concerns your uncle.'

'It gave him a perfect excuse to send Burke and his men to Hidden Valley. They were supposed to bring Big Shaun Rogan back with them. My uncle wanted to lay down the law to him.'

'And in their natural disappointment at finding him away from home, they contented themselves with brutally assaulting his wife and one of his sons,' Clay said. 'Does your uncle approve of Burke's methods?'

'He encourages them,' she said drily. 'I'm afraid he classes the Irish with the negroes – both races being naturally inferior to his own and conceived that way by God.'

'Sir George must indeed be a man of penetrating intelligence,' Clay observed. 'Might I enquire whether you sympathize with his views?'

'As my grandmother on my mother's side was a Hindu, born and raised in Calcutta, you might say I'm prejudiced,' she told him.

They walked their horses along the track, allowing the animals to choose their own pace and Clay glanced sideways at her. The mixed blood was plain in the large, almond-shaped eyes and the creamy skin peculiar to Eurasian women.

She turned and, finding him looking at her, flushed. For the moment, her self-assurance seemed to desert her and she became simply a young eighteen-year-old girl with a rather boyish charm. Then she smiled shyly and in that brief moment of revelation, he knew she was the most beautiful thing he had ever seen in his life. A queer, inexplicable tenderness flooded through him. He reached across and squeezed her hand reassuringly, and her smile seemed to deepen, to become luminous, and she no longer looked afraid, but completely sure of herself.

At that moment, the rain increased into a monsoon-like downpour and she spurred her horse forward with a gay laugh. Clay gave Pegeen her head and galloped after her. She turned her horse off the track and rode down into a small wooded valley, and through the trees he caught a gleam of water.

She stopped in the shelter of a huge beech tree whose roots reached down to the edge of a small, quiet pool, and as he dismounted, she slid to the ground.

She pushed a damp tendril of dark hair away from her forehead. 'We'll be safe here until it eases up a little.'

Clay took out a cheroot and lit it, while she threw pieces of twig into the water with an absorbed look on her face and snapped her fingers as a duck swirled across the water, expecting to be fed.

A small wind blew from the other side, bringing with it the dank, wet smell of rotting leaves. 'That smell,' she said, turning toward him, her face vibrant with emotion, 'Isn't it wonderful? Doesn't it make you feel good to be alive?'

He nodded. 'My favourite season, the fall. Always something a little sad about it, though. Old dreams like smoke in the air, still lingering for a brief moment before disappearing forever.'

It was impossible for him to keep the bitterness from his voice as he thought of his own dream, the dreams of thousands like him, which had ended with the Confederacy at Appomattox.

She placed a hand on his arm and said gently, 'I'm sorry, I was forgetting what this year has brought you.'

He managed a wry smile. 'I thought it had at last brought me peace, but I've found precious little of it in Ireland so far. Tell me, what were you doing so close to the Rogan place? It's hardly good weather for riding.'

'I intended going to Claremont to see you,' she said. 'There's a sick child in the village – a little boy. I wondered if you would have a look at him. There isn't a doctor nearer than Galway.'

'Surely you chose a roundabout way of going to Claremont?'

She smiled. 'One of the servants overheard my uncle giving Burke his orders and told me. I rode over to warn the Rogans. They're friends of mine – good friends.'

With an abrupt and almost childlike gesture, she reached up and traced a finger along the sabre scar that sliced his cheek. 'When did you get that?'

He shrugged. 'A long time ago – a thousand years ago. Pittsburgh Landing.'

A slight frown creased her forehead and then it cleared. 'Oh, yes, I was forgetting you had different names for some of the battles. The Yankees called it Shiloh, didn't they?'

She was full of surprises, he thought. 'You seem to know your facts.'

She nodded. 'I read Fremont's diary of his visit to the Confederate Army when it was published in London two years ago.'

'He certainly covered some ground in three months,' Clay said. 'But he left in the summer of sixty-three after Gettysburg.'

'I also read Mr Lawley's letters from the Southern States which appeared regularly in *The Times*,' she continued. 'And then your uncle used to give me the war news from your father's letters. Unfortunately, there weren't very many of them and I only know of some of your exploits. I'm hoping you'll fill in the gaps for me.'

He laughed. 'Perhaps, but at a later date. I'm much more interested in you at the moment.'

She shrugged. 'There isn't much to tell. My father was a captain in a regiment of sepoys. I was born in Madras, but when the Mutiny started, we were living in Lucknow, where my father was stationed. We took refuge in the Residency. My father was killed during the siege, my mother died two months later.'

'Had you no other relatives?'

She shook her head. 'My uncle is my legal guardian. I was left well provided for, so I'm no financial burden. However, remembering my grandmother, he treats me with the greatest respect and a rather frigid courtesy. Most of the time, he tries to believe I'm not there.'

'And what about Burke?' Clay said.

She frowned and an expression of distaste appeared on her face. 'My uncle's health isn't too good. He spends most of the time in the conservatory with his flowers and leaves the handling of the estate to Burke.'

'You don't seem to have much time for him,' Clay said.

'I loathe him. He was born and raised on the estate and he's utterly ruthless. He's determined to achieve position in the world and he has already foresworn his own people to do it. He's the most hated and feared man in the district.'

'The men who rode with him this morning were certainly an ugly-looking crowd,' Clay said.

She nodded. 'Lowland Scots, especially imported to do my uncle's dirty work.'

'Does he approve of the methods Burke uses?'

'He's not interested in methods, Colonel, only in results,' Joanna Hamilton said drily. She looked up at the sky, which had lightened a little. 'I think we'd better be going. The rain seems to have slackened.'

Clay helped her into the saddle, and as he turned away, she urged her horse forward and cried, 'I'll race you back.'

He swung a leg over Pegeen and followed her up through the trees and galloped along the track. When he came out into the open expanse of the moor, she was a good forty or fifty yards in front of him and he leaned low over Pegeen's neck and urged her on. Gradually, he grew closer and then they were racing alongside each other. She turned and gave him a flashing smile and, suddenly, he felt absurdly happy.

He gave Pegeen her head and plunged down through the scattering of trees at the back of Claremont and entered the courtyard. When Joanna Hamilton arrived a few moments later, he was already dismounted and waiting for her.

She laughed gaily and cried out in mock anger. 'It was no fair match, sir. You were mounted on the finest mare in the county.'

He helped her down from the saddle, a slight smile on his face. 'The finest mare and the most beautiful woman. What more could a man ask?'

For the second time that day, she flushed and could think of nothing to say in reply, and Clay turned to speak to Joshua who had appeared in the doorway. 'Joshua, this is Miss Hamilton. It's to her good offices we owe our welcome last night.'

Joanna Hamilton held out her hand with a completely natural gesture and Joshua took it, a smile of approval on his face. 'My pleasure, ma'am.' He turned to Clay. 'There's coffee freshly prepared, if you and Miss Hamilton would care for a cup.'

Clay looked enquiringly at Joanna, who nodded, and they went inside. Joshua said, 'A letter was delivered by one of Sir George Hamilton's men an hour ago. I've put it on the table.'

Clay excused himself and opened the envelope, while Joshua poured the coffee. After a while, he looked up and smiled. 'Your uncle is holding a small reception this evening to welcome me to the district. Did you know about this?'

She sipped her coffee and nodded coolly. 'But of course. I've had the preparations in hand for two days now. In such matters, he leaves everything to my judgment. I flatter myself I've never let him down yet. An invitation to a Hamilton affair is never refused.'

Clay nodded slowly. 'I see. How many guests are expected?'

'Between fifty and sixty, depending on the weather and the state of the roads. Will you accept?'

'As you will be there, how could I refuse?' he said gravely.

For a brief moment, they gazed at each other silently, and then she smiled and picked up her gloves. 'If you don't mind, I think we should be making a move. I've a great deal to do back at the house and this business in the village will take us another hour.'

He excused himself and went upstairs for his bag. When he came down again, she was already mounted and waiting for him, Joshua standing at Pegeen's head.

Clay swung up into the saddle. 'I shouldn't be longer than an hour and a half,' he said.

Joshua nodded and went back inside, and Clay and the girl moved round to the front of the house and cantered down the drive to the main road.

It was still raining heavily when they rode into

Drumore, and he decided he had seldom seen a more dismal sight in his life than the village, with its unpaved street and wretched cottages squatting in the mud.

There was a well in the centre of the street, and as they approached, a woman was in the act of lifting a pail of water down to the ground. She leaned against the parapet for a moment, as if tired, and then bent wearily to pick up her pail.

Clay stepped down to the ground with an oath and hurried toward her. She was in an advanced state of pregnancy, her belly swollen, face blotched and ugly.

He took the pail from her hand and said gently, 'You shouldn't be at such work, you'll do yourself an injury.'

She shrugged hopelessly. 'Who else will if I don't?'

'Why, I will!' Clay told her. 'Which is your cottage?'

She pointed silently across the street and he walked before her and opened the door. He found himself in a dark, miserable room. The stone walls streamed with moisture and the only warmth came from a turf fire which smouldered in the wide hearth. An old woman stirred something in a large iron pot and ignored him. His nose wrinkled in disgust and he put down the pail and went back outside.

Joanna still sat her horse and smiled down at the woman. 'Colonel Fitzgerald is a doctor, Mrs Cooney. If you need his help when the baby is due, you've only to send to Claremont.'

The woman turned to him enquiringly, and he nodded. 'Any time of the day or night, Mrs Cooney. Send a message and I'll come running.'

Sudden tears appeared in her eyes. She seized his hand and held it to her face for a moment and then rushed into the cottage and closed the door behind her.

As he climbed back into the saddle, there was disgust on his face. 'That cottage is little better than a kennel. What chance does she have of bringing a child into the world under such conditions? Who owns the place?'

'My uncle,' she told him. 'Only the Rogans own their own land in this district, and you, of course.'

'Then, by God, he should be ashamed to call himself a man,' Clay said. 'And I'll damn well tell him so when we meet.'

'You'll be wasting your breath,' she told him. 'He won't know what on earth you're talking about. Don't forget he classes the Irish with the negroes.'

'Then I'll tell him I've seen slaves better treated.'

'But the slaves were worth money,' she told him. 'There lies the difference.'

She reined in outside a cottage on the outskirts of the village and Clay dismounted and helped her to the ground. As he unstrapped his bag, the door opened and a priest emerged.

He was a small-boned, fragile man in his sixties, with a shock of grey hair falling untidily over his brow. His face was lined and careworn, but the eyes which turned toward Clay were blue and sparkling and full of faith.

'This is Colonel Fitzgerald,' Joanna said. 'Colonel, Father Costello.'

The priest smiled and shook hands, his grip firm. 'Your uncle and I were great friends, Colonel, and I knew your father, but that was many years ago. I'm glad you've come.'

He went back into the cottage and Clay and Joanna followed him. It was almost an exact replica of the other one, the walls beaded with moisture and the room half-filled with acrid smoke from the turf fire. Chickens roosted in the rafters and a goat was tethered to the wall.

In one corner was a large bed covered with a tattered counterpane, in another a straw palliasse upon the floor. The boy was lying upon it, a filthy blanket over him, and a woman sat upon a small stool beside him.

The sounds of the child's breathing were horribly familiar and Clay's heart sank as he dropped down onto one knee and examined him. The skin was so pale that it seemed almost transparent, the flesh moulding the bones so that the cheeks were deep hollows. His shirt was stained with blood, and as Clay placed a hand on his forehead, the frail body was racked by a spasm of violent coughing that was followed by a sudden rush of blood from the mouth.

Behind him the woman sobbed, as he gently sponged the blood away with a cloth. When the boy's face was clean, Clay opened his bag and took out a small bottle of laudanum. He asked for a cup of water, and after a moment, Joanna handed one to him.

Clay poured several drops of the laudanum into the water, raised the boy's head and made him drink the mixture. Then he got to his feet and turned, his face grave. 'He should sleep for several hours without waking. How many times has he emitted blood?'

'Only God knows, sir,' the woman replied. 'He cannot eat, and at night his whole body breaks out in a great sweat. Even when his father and I take him into bed to warm him, he still shivers.'

She dissolved into tears and Clay patted her gently on the shoulder. 'Try not to worry too much. He'll sleep quietly tonight, I promise you. I'll call in again tomorrow.'

Her face worked convulsively. 'But we can't pay you, sir. God help us but we've no money.'

Clay shook his head quickly. 'My services won't cost you a penny.' Before she could reply, he pulled open the door and went outside, too full to speak.

Joanna appeared at his shoulder, her face grave. 'Can you do anything?'

He shook his head. 'It's one of the most advanced cases of consumption I've ever seen. How the boy managed to survive this long, I'll never know. If he lives another twenty-four hours, I'll be surprised. If there's any pity for suffering humanity in this universe, he'll not wake from that drugged sleep.'

'It is God's will,' Father Costello said quietly.

Clay swung into the saddle and gathered the

reins in his right hand. 'It depends how you look at it, Father. I prefer to think that the boy never stood a chance from the day he was conceived, because he was born in a pigsty and raised in conditions I would consider inadequate for my horse.'

He turned to Joanna, his face hard. 'If you'll excuse me, I'll leave you here. What I need at the moment is a drink. I'll see you tonight.' He quickly moved away before she could reply and cantered up the street to Cohan's public house.

He had his drink and then another, and as he rode back to Claremont half an hour later, the memory of the child's wasted face had temporarily lost its clarity.

4

It was a fine warm evening, but rather oppressive, and there was more than a touch of thunder in the air as the coach turned in through the great iron gates and moved rapidly along the broad carriageway toward Drumore House.

Clay leaned out of the window and examined the place with interest. It was a late Georgian mansion surrounded by superb ornamental gardens, and already the windows were a blaze of lights. As Joshua halted the coach exactly at the bottom of the steps leading up to the front entrance, two footmen hurried forward and one of them opened the coach door for Clay to step down.

He paused in the portico to look out over the grounds toward the road. The sky was as yellow as brass, and beyond the black mass of the trees, smoke ascended in a straight line from the chimney of the lodge. It was almost like stepping back into another world, a world of comfort and gracious living that had died with the war, and he sighed and passed through into a wide hall.

A footman took his hat and cloak, and Clay handed his invitation to a tall, greying butler, who examined it impassively and bowed. 'Sir George is waiting for you in the conservatory, Colonel Fitzgerald. This way, sir.'

Clay followed him along a broad, carpeted corridor to a green baize door, which the butler opened. They moved through an alien world of damp heat and strange plants. Broad green leaves and twisted vines formed an archway over the path and weird, brightly coloured flowers he had never seen before grew in profusion everywhere.

In the centre of the conservatory, there was a clearing in which stood a basket-work table and several chairs. A man in evening dress was engaged in pruning a vine, his hands covered by leather gloves.

'Colonel Fitzgerald is here, Sir George,' the butler informed him.

'Thank you, Hammond. Tell my niece we'll be

with her in half an hour.' The voice was dry and precise and he spoke without turning round.

The butler withdrew and Clay sat on the edge of the table. 'I trust you'll forgive me, Colonel,' Sir George said. 'I'm engaged in rather a delicate task.' Almost in the same moment, he gave a sigh of satisfaction and turned, stripping the gloves from his hands.

He was in his early sixties, tall and cadaverous with sunken eyes in a thin face, and the hand he extended was limp and flaccid to the touch. His smile was of the briefest and hardly disturbed his frosty countenance. 'Welcome to Drumore, Colonel. A pleasure to have you as a guest in my home.'

The sentiment was so courteous that Clay found it impossible to reply except in the same way. 'I'm sure you'll understand my reason for declining your invitation to spend last night with you. I was in something of a hurry to see Claremont.'

'Perfectly understandable, Colonel,' Sir George said. 'You'll join me in a glass of sherry, I hope?' As he filled two glasses from a decanter, he went on, 'I believe you and my agent were involved in some unpleasantness this morning. You must allow me to apologize. Burke is inclined to be a little rough at times. Unfortunately our situation here is such that under present conditions, such methods are the only ones which seem to work.'

'And what exactly is your situation?' Clay asked, as he sipped a little of his sherry.

'But you've seen some of it already for yourself,' Sir George told him. 'In what civilized country today is highway robbery commonplace, and murder and every other conceivable kind of outrage a regular occurrence?'

Clay nodded slowly. 'I give you that, but surely one must look for the cause of all this. Doesn't it lie in the misery and squalor of the people and their desire for Home Rule?'

Sir George shrugged. 'Home Rule is an economic impossibility. We need the power and protection of the British Empire. Ask any of the landowners you'll meet here tonight for an honest and sensible answer. They'll all agree with me.'

'I have met those who wouldn't,' Clay told him.

'The Rogans?' Sir George frowned slightly. 'A violent and troublemaking family, notorious throughout the county. The constabulary have been trying to lay them by the heels for years. If you'll take my advice, you'll prosecute over this affair on the Galway Road.'

Clay shook his head. 'The whole thing turned out to be nothing more than a boyish prank. Full restitution has been made and there's an end to it.'

'Might I ask why you were visiting the Rogans this morning?' Sir George said.

Some inner caution made Clay reply, 'I was merely out for a ride. I arrived at the head of the valley in time to see your men using Mrs Rogan and one of her sons rather harshly. Naturally, I intervened.'

'But these people are savages.'

Clay started to protest, and Sir George raised a hand to silence him. 'No, let me tell you a story and then judge for yourself.'

He sat down in one of the chairs and poured another glass of sherry, his face perfectly calm. 'Fifteen years ago, we were going through just such a period as this. Several landowners had been murdered and no man seemed to be safe. I prided myself I had always been fair and honest with my own tenants, and because of that, disregarded the threats on my life made in several letters I received.'

'Who were those letters from?' Clay asked.

Sir George opened a drawer in the table, and taking out a folded sheet of paper, passed it across.

'That's an example of the sort of thing I mean. It was found pinned to the front door the other morning.'

The message was short and to the point and inscribed in neat block letters.

YOUR TURN WILL COME SOON. LOOK FOR ME.
CAPTAIN SWING.

'Who is this Captain Swing?' Clay said, handing it back.

Sir George permitted himself a contemptuous smile. 'There is no such individual, Colonel. They amuse themselves with their secret societies and romantic names. Captain Swing, Captain Moonlight – such names are used by every disaffected rogue who feels like writing a threatening letter to his landlord.'

'Presumably during the previous trouble, these threats were put into action,' Clay said.

Sir George nodded. 'My wife and I had been visiting some friends. Rather foolishly as it turned out, we rode home alone together in a gig. It was a fine summer evening and as I drove, she chatted to me about some improvements she intended to make in the garden.'

He seemed to find some difficulty in speaking,

and for a moment, there was a pause while Clay waited, guessing what was to come.

Sir George emptied his glass and placed it carefully upon the table. 'The assassin was lying in wait in a small wood on the hillside above the bridge, a mile along the Galway Road from the main gates. He only fired once and the bullet, which was intended for me, killed my wife instantly.'

Clay sighed and said softly, 'So violence breeds violence.'

'Perhaps it does,' Sir George said. 'But you must surely see my point of view, Colonel? The risk that his shot might miss me and kill my wife must have been obvious to the assassin, and yet he took it. Can you really expect me to have any feeling other than hate for these people, after such a deed?'

Clay shook his head. 'No, it's perfectly understandable, but perhaps a more enlightened attitude on the part of the landlords as a whole would go a long way toward stamping out this sort of thing. I visited a dying boy, riddled with consumption, this morning. He lives in one of your cottages in the village. I've never seen such a pest-hole. How can you expect people who live in such conditions to be anything other than violent and lawless?'

'But the standards one would apply in England

cannot be applied here. These people are animals.' An expression of disbelief appeared on Clay's face, and Sir George went on, 'I'll tell you another true story and you can judge for yourself. Two years ago, a young Englishman – Lord Craig – was left an estate near here. When he arrived to examine the property, he was disgusted to find that most of the peasantry lived in one-roomed cottages without chimneys or any kind of sanitation. He spent a great deal of money in having a model village constructed, and after his tenants had moved into the new cottages, he had the old ones pulled down.'

'What happened then?' Clay asked.

'Within a month, a deputation waited upon him to ask him to have the chimney shafts blocked up. They complained at the loss of heat. When Lord Craig visited the cottages in connection with this request, he discovered to his horror, that his tenants were indulging in all their old habits. Sharing the living quarters with livestock and poultry and using a bucket in the corner of the room in preference to the privies at the end of the garden.'

'What did he do about it?' Clay said.

Sir George smiled thinly. 'He sold the estate to me and returned to England a sadder but wiser man.'

'But these things take time,' Clay said.

Sir George shook his head. 'I can see that only experience will teach you. You'll find out for yourself before you have been here for three months.'

'I'm not even sure I shall stay that long,' Clay told him.

Sir George raised his eyebrows in surprise. 'You don't intend to make your home here, then?'

Clay shook his head. 'For me, this is merely a sentimental journey I couldn't resist taking.'

'Then I trust you will bear in mind my offer for your property. I think you'll find it more than a fair one.'

Before Clay could reply, Sir George's face was racked by a spasm of pain. He clapped a hand to his mouth and moved quickly toward a stone sink which stood against the wall. As he reached it, a quantity of brown vomit erupted from his mouth and he leaned over the edge of the sink, his thin shoulders working convulsively.

Finally, he straightened up and turned, wiping his mouth with a handkerchief. 'I must apologize, Colonel. Most unpleasant for you.'

'You forget I'm a doctor.' Clay worked the pump handle up and down several times, flushing the vomit away, and filled one of the glasses with water. 'Drink this and tell me how often you have such attacks.'

Sir George rinsed his mouth and spat it into the sink. 'Come now, Colonel. As a medical man, I'm sure you've already made your diagnosis. For my part, I received my sentence from the finest physicians in London last year. The cancer is in the stomach and there is nothing to be done.'

'I would have guessed as much from your appearance alone,' Clay told him. He hesitated and then said, 'If there is anything I can do, don't hesitate to call on me at any time.'

Sir George shook his head and said tranquilly, 'I have a very good man in Galway who visits me every couple of weeks. No one could do more. You would oblige me by not mentioning this to my niece, though. I see no reason to distress her unnecessarily.' He smiled. 'And now I think we really should be joining the others. My guests will be wondering what has become of me.'

As they moved through the conservatory and out into the passage, Clay considered what had happened, a frown upon his face. He had come here prepared to despise this man and had ended in pitying him.

Life at times could be extremely confusing, he decided, as a footman opened the door for them and they passed into a long, narrow room filled with people.

There was a slight, excited murmur of conversation as heads turned toward them, and he noticed with some surprise that Burke was standing on his own against the wall, conventionally attired in evening wear. Sir George led Clay through the crowd, stopping here and there to make introductions. Finally he excused himself, leaving Clay in the centre of an admiring group of extravagantly uniformed Hussar officers from the garrison at Galway.

Someone pressed a glass of champagne into his hand, and a young captain called Vale said, 'I see you have been wounded, Colonel, and yet we were given to understand that surgeons were treated as non-combatants by both sides.'

'Someone must have forgotten to tell the Yankees,' Clay said and there was general laughter. As it died down he went on, 'The situation changed somewhat as the war progressed. Circumstances forced me into becoming a general officer. I had to combine the role of surgeon when it was needed – which was often,' he added ruefully.

There was more laughter and someone said, 'We were all under the impression that the South would win the war, Colonel. To what do you attribute her defeat?'

Clay shrugged. 'The Confederacy was doomed from the beginning. It's impossible to march in the face of history or progress, gentlemen. Unfortunately, this usually only becomes apparent in retrospect.'

'Did you command a regiment of cavalry, then, Colonel?' Vale enquired.

'Colonel Fitzgerald commanded two regiments of Georgia cavalry and a brigade at Five Forks, but ten days later the Confederacy had ceased to exist and his promotion to brigadier was never ratified.' The group parted to allow Joanna Hamilton to pass through. 'You see, I do know about you, Colonel.' She smiled and took Clay's arm. 'Shall we go in to dinner?'

As they walked toward the dining room, he noticed their reflections in the large, gilt-framed mirror upon the wall. Joanna looked enchanting in a crinoline of white silk, her waist so slender he could almost have spanned it with his two hands.

He himself was conventionally attired in black,

his only distinguishing mark the ruffled shirt commonly worn in Georgia on such occasions. No one in all honesty could ever call him handsome, he decided, but by God, they made a presentable couple, and then Joanna's eyes met his in the mirror. Her mouth quivered slightly, and the fan came up to cover her face as they went into the dining room.

He sat between Joanna and her uncle throughout the meal, enjoying the superb food and listening to the flow of idle chatter on either side. Sir George Hamilton ate sparingly, which was to be expected, and seemed to contribute little to the conversation. Finally, the ladies withdrew and the port was passed round.

Clay lit a cheroot and sat in silence listening to the conversation of others. It consisted in the main of a discussion of the present uneasy state of affairs throughout the country, with various suggestions as to how it might be remedied.

Most of the landowners present seemed to favour a harsher treatment of the peasantry, the strengthening of local garrisons and the introduction of martial law.

One man even suggested that every tenth male in each village might be arrested and held as a hostage against the good behaviour of his fellows. The unfortunate wretches chosen were apparently to be hanged if any further lawless acts took place within their own particular community.

Clay had assumed that the man who proposed the idea was speaking lightly, until he heard the murmur of approval which rose on every side and someone said, 'Hang one of these swine to every tree between here and Galway. Only way to cure 'em. Wish I could lay hands on the rogue who sent me this.'

A sheet of paper was tossed into the centre of the table and someone picked it up. It was passed from hand to hand with angry murmurs, and when it reached Clay, he saw that it was another threatening letter signed Captain Swing, but in a different hand.

The man who had spoken was a gross, evil-looking creature with podgy hands and permanently wet lips. There was something obscene about him, and as they rose to join the ladies, Captain Vale moved to Clay's shoulder and said, 'I see you're admiring friend Marley, Colonel.'

'Who is he?' Clay asked.

'Owns a large estate about ten miles from here on the road to Galway. A place called Kileen.' Vale made a face. 'A revolting individual. I'm surprised Sir George invited him.'

'Presumably he wasn't joking when he said he'd like to hang a man from every tree between here and Galway?' Clay said.

'Marley never jokes about anything, Colonel,' Vale assured him. 'He rules his tenants with a rod of iron and treats them like animals.' They helped themselves to brandy from a salver which was being carried round by a footman, and Vale continued. 'He has a penchant for young girls. Anything between thirteen and eighteen suits him. After that they're too old.'

'Presumably he has a plentiful supply. He seems happy enough with life at the moment.'

Vale nodded grimly. 'As I remarked, his tenants have to do as they are told. One of these days, someone will shoot him from behind a hedge and I'll be called in to hunt the poor devil down.'

'Personally, I'd be inclined to give the man concerned a medal and book him a passage to America,' Clay said.

'Under the circumstances, I'm inclined to agree with you. Marley's parties are like something out of a nightmare. Only the scum of the countryside will attend. His favourite trick is to have one of the girls stripped and hunted through the grounds by torchlight, the whole drunken mob howling at her heels. You can imagine what the prize is for the first one to catch her.'

Clay took him by the arm and led him toward the buffet table. 'After that final slice of information, I really do need another drink.'

A moment later, a small string ensemble, especially brought from Galway for the occasion, struck up a Strauss waltz. Clay excused himself and crossed the room to where Joanna was engaged in giving some instructions to the butler.

'My dance, I think,' he said, with a slight bow.

She consulted her card, brow furrowed. 'I'm awfully sorry, Colonel Fitzgerald, but you should have come earlier. I'm afraid I've only been able to keep a dozen dances open for you.'

Laughter erupted from his throat, so that people standing near at hand turned as he took her arm and led her onto the floor.

They danced well together, and as they circled the room she looked up into his face and smiled. 'You look extremely handsome tonight.'

He grimaced and shook his head. 'I have been accused of many things, Miss Hamilton, but never of being handsome.'

She frowned in genuine puzzlement. 'Surely you must be aware that every woman in the room is longing to have you dance with her?'

Before he could think of a suitable reply, the music died away and people stopped dancing. There were shocked gasps, and somewhere, a woman stifled a scream in her throat.

The French windows leading out onto the terrace had been opened a little earlier because of the warmth of the evening. Standing just inside the room were two men who had obviously stepped out of the darkness.

The one on the left was Kevin Rogan, and he carried a shotgun under one arm, thumbs hooked carelessly into his broad leather belt. His eyes swept over the crowd and met Clay's and something like a smile touched his lip.

It was not difficult to guess the identity of his companion. Shaun Rogan was one of the largest men Clay had ever seen. He must have been all of six feet four or five, with a great breadth of shoulder, and his hair was a snow-white mane swept back behind his ears. He wore a felt hat and corduroy jacket.

Complete silence descended upon the room as Sir George walked forward to face him. 'I don't know what you're doing here, Rogan,' he said calmly, 'but I'd like to remind you that this is my property. As I have not invited you here, you're guilty of trespassing. I suggest you leave as quickly as you came.'

Shaun Rogan's voice was like the tuck of a drum. 'Trespassing, is it, George Hamilton? And what was it your men were doing this morning when they invaded my land and assaulted not only one of my sons, but also my wife? Is it a woman-beater ye are now?'

Burke had moved to a position directly behind his master's shoulder and he now took a quick step forward. Sir George held him back with one arm. 'I want no trouble in front of my guests, Rogan. If you have a legitimate complaint, take it to the constabulary in Galway.'

'Would you listen to him?' Shaun Rogan demanded, looking round the room. 'And what chance would I have against the likes of him?' There was no answer and he shook his head. 'No, I've no complaint to make, but I've got a warning for you and your pet lap-dog hiding there behind your shoulder. If you as much as set foot on my land again, you'll get a bullet in you and there's my solemn promise on it.'

He started to turn away, and Sir George's anger got the better of him. 'By God, you go too far, Rogan,' he cried, face suffused with passion. 'I'll see you rot in Galway gaol yet, you scum.'

Rogan turned slowly. 'Scum, is it?' he said softly. 'And what name would ye give to a man, who wanting a quarrel, hasn't the guts to face his enemy himself, but sends his bully boys to manhandle a sixty-year-old woman?'

There was complete silence in the room and Joanna's breath hissed softly between her teeth. Rogan slipped a hand into his coat and pulled out a pistol which he threw down at his enemy's feet.

'There, you dog,' he said harshly. 'Here's as good a chance as you'll ever get to rid the world of me, and ye haven't the guts to take it.'

He turned his back and, pushing Kevin before him, moved to the French windows. In that same instant, Burke dropped to one knee and reached for the pistol. He thumbed back the hammer and levelled it, still kneeling. As he pulled the trigger, Clay moved. He stamped downwards and the pistol exploded harmlessly into the floor. Burke dropped it with a cry of pain and clutched his wrist.

Kevin swung, shotgun levelled to fire, but his

father moved quickly to stay him. His eyes met Clay's and Kevin murmured something softly to him. A slight smile appeared on Shaun Rogan's grim face, and he nodded and said, 'I'm obliged to you, Colonel.' For a moment longer they stood there in the light and then they melted away into the darkness

Sir George turned to Clay and his face was calm, although a muscle pulled at the corner of his right eye, betraying his inner agitation. 'I must thank you for acting so promptly, Colonel. Burke's action was understandable but ill-advised. You have saved us all considerable unpleasantness.'

He raised his voice and said to the room in general, 'Please do not let this unfortunate affair interfere with your enjoyment, ladies and gentlemen.' He nodded to the pianist, and as the ensemble struck up a waltz, walked from the room, Burke at his heels.

People stood in groups, their heads together as they discussed what had happened, and Clay gave his arm to Joanna and they moved out through the French windows onto the terrace.

Joanna leaned against a balustrade and gave a long sigh of relief. 'Thank God you managed to stop him in time. If Shaun Rogan had been killed here tonight, the scandal would have rocked the country.'

'Why does your uncle hate him so much?'

She shrugged. 'I don't really know. Ask me why he hates so many things. I think it's because Big Shaun has always refused to bow the knee. He's like a rock, immovable, and my uncle doesn't like that. He likes to think he can bend people to his will.'

'But he isn't always successful, is he?' Clay said. 'I wonder what he'd say if he knew his niece was addicted to moonlight gallops dressed like a man.'

She laughed lightly. 'What he doesn't know can never hurt him.' She shivered. 'It's turned rather chilly. Do you mind if we go back inside?'

As they entered the room, a young Hussar officer approached and claimed Joanna for a dance, and Clay went across to the buffet and helped himself to a large brandy. As he was drinking it, Vale came up, an expression of disgust on his face. 'You look as though you could do with a drink,' Clay said.

Vale nodded. 'I've just been listening to that swine Marley boasting about his latest affair. He's as drunk as a lord, of course. It seems he's got some wretched girl locked up in a room back at his house. Her mother's a widow and he threatened to evict her for arrears of rent. The girl came this afternoon to plead with him and he made his terms pretty plain. Apparently, she turned him down flat and he locked her up, to give her time to consider the consequences, as he so delicately phrases it.'

He swallowed some brandy and excused himself as another dance started, and Clay turned away and stared out of the window, anger rising in him. He reached for the decanter, filled his glass to the brim and drained it, the brandy spreading through his body like liquid fire. Then he felt a hand on his sleeve and Joanna was beside him.

Her smile faded as she saw his face. 'What is it, Clay?' she said. 'What's happened?'

He laughed harshly. 'Why nothing. I suddenly feel in need of a little fresh air, that's all.'

He beckoned to one of the footmen and asked to have his carriage brought round to the front door, and Joanna grasped his arm and said in a whisper, 'Clay, I'm frightened. You look like the Devil himself.'

He smiled reassuringly. 'Don't worry about me, my dear. I'm subject to these moods now and then. What I need is a gallop to blow the cobwebs away.'

She came with him to the door and he collected his cloak and hat. As they moved out onto the steps, she smiled up at him, face pale in the lamplight. 'I'll see you again?'

He took her hands in his and held them for a moment. 'Try and keep me away.'

Her face broke into a radiant smile and she moved very close and said softly, 'Don't do anything foolish, Clay.'

He turned away down the steps, and as he climbed into his coach, one of the footmen said to a groom who lounged against the wall, 'Mr Marley wants his coach to be ready for eleven.'

For a moment, Clay paused as he watched the footman run back up the steps and enter the house, and then he knew, with complete surety, what he had to do. He hammered on the roof with his fist and Joshua whipped up the horses and took them away in a burst of speed.

5

When they reached Claremont, he went straight up to his bedroom and started to change. As he pulled on his riding boots, Joshua appeared in the doorway.

'You intend to go out again, Colonel?' he said.

Clay nodded. 'You can saddle the mare, but first get that map I purchased the day we landed and find Kileen for me. If I remember rightly, we passed through it on the way here yesterday.'

Joshua opened the brown valise and produced a linen-backed map, which he spread on the bed. 'I've got it, Colonel,' he said, after a moment. 'About nine or ten miles from here.'

Clay moved beside him. 'There should be a large estate nearby. It belongs to a man called Marley.'

Joshua glanced up, surprise on his face. 'They were taking about him in the servants' hall tonight. His coachman was there. Some of the stories left a bad taste.'

Clay laughed grimly. 'I had the doubtful pleasure of meeting the gentleman in person. You can believe anything you were told about him. Now saddle the mare. I haven't much time.'

Joshua left the room and Clay examined the map. After a while, he gave a grunt of satisfaction. A track was marked which cut straight across the moor at the back of Drumore House, joining the Galway Road a mile from Kileen, shortening the distance considerably.

He folded the map and opened the leather travelling trunk which stood against the wall. After a moment, he found what he was looking for – his old felt campaign hat and the shabby grey military greatcoat with the caped shoulders which had served him so well during the last two years of the Confederacy.

He buttoned the coat up to his chin and belted the Dragoon Colt in its black leather holster about his waist. Finally, he pulled the brim of his hat down over his eyes and examined himself.

In the dim light of the oil lamps, a ghost stared

out of the mirror, a man who had died the night before Appomattox. In some strange way, it was like meeting an old friend. For a moment, he was conscious of a feeling that was close to nostalgia and his mind jumped back into a past which was so near and yet so incredibly far away.

He sighed and opening a drawer in the tallboy, took out a black silk scarf, which he knotted behind his neck and pulled up over his face. The effect was startling. The man who now stood there in the shadows was a stranger, full of menace and utterly dangerous.

It was as if another person stared out at him, someone over whom he had no control, and for a moment he hesitated, a queer coldness seeping through him, while inside a tiny warning voice seemed to tell him to draw back before it was too late. But only for a moment. He pulled down the scarf, bowed mockingly at his reflection and, turning on his heel, left the room.

Joshua waited in the courtyard, one hand gently rubbing Pegeen's muzzle. She whinnied softly with pleasure when Clay appeared and swung up into the saddle. 'I'm not sure how long I'll be,' he said. 'It all depends on friend Marley.'

'I've seen that look on your face before,' Joshua

said. 'Presumably you don't intend to pay him a social call.' He hesitated and then continued. 'Excuse me if I'm talking out of turn, Colonel, but what happened back there? Did Mr Marley insult you?'

'I think you could call it that,' Clay said.

'Then you aren't visiting him for the sake of his health?'

'I wouldn't say so,' Clay told him. 'In fact, I may very probably have to shoot him before the night is out.' He clicked his tongue, and Pegeen moved quickly across the courtyard and took the path which led up toward the rim of the valley.

The night was clean and fresh, the darkness perfumed with the scent of gorse and the faint indefinable touch of autumn lay over the land, drifting up from the valleys below like wood smoke, filling him with a nervous excitement.

The track lay clear and white in the moonlight as he gave Pegeen her head and galloped across the moor and the lower slopes of the hills.

Somewhere, laughter sounded faintly through the darkness, gay and carefree, touching him with an envious sadness, and he turned Pegeen onto the turf and moved forward at a careful walk. Drumore House lay below in the valley, still bright with lights, and music drifted up toward him.

He paused for a moment in the trees and listened. It was an old familiar waltz, sad and gay in the same breath, with love and tender laughter in every line of it. He had last heard it in the month before the war began.

For a moment, time ceased to have any meaning, and he was back again in Georgia, arriving rather late for a ball to celebrate the coming-of-age of the sister of his best friend. Ahead lay a week of hunting and parties, and beyond that, the long, golden years.

As his father had often told him, it never paid to count on anything in this world. He sighed once for the summer that had gone and urged Pegeen through the trees and back onto the track. As the music faded into the night, he broke into a gallop again.

Half an hour later he moved down onto the Galway Road and cantered toward Kileen. He splashed through a wide ford and walked Pegeen through the sleeping village.

Kileen House was two hundred yards on the other side, a black mass rearing out of the night, and he turned in through the gates and came to a halt before the front door.

A light showed in the hall, but otherwise the place was in complete darkness. He mounted the steps and pulled the bell chain. The sound jangled faintly in the hidden depths of the house and its echo was from another world.

After a while, steps approached and he pulled the scarf up over his face and drew his revolver. As the door started to open, he pushed his way in and closed it behind him.

The man who faced him was old and round-shouldered in a shabby frock coat, skin yellow and wrinkled with age. His eyes widened in terror and his mouth opened in a cry of alarm.

Clay seized him by the throat and deliberately roughened his voice. 'One word and you're a dead man. Who are you?'

He released his grip slightly and the old man replied in a cracked voice, 'Only the butler, sir. God save us, if it's Mr Marley you want, he's not at home.'

'Who else is here?' Clay demanded.

'The servants, sir, but they're all abed at the back of the house.'

'You're forgetting the young woman who came to see your master this afternoon,' Clay told him. 'Where is she?'

'Eithne Fallon, you mean, sir?' The old man was shaking with fright as he picked up the lamp from a nearby table. 'This way, sir. This way.'

Clay followed him across the hall and they mounted a wide staircase. The old man moved along the landing and paused outside a door at the far end. He produced a bunch of keys from his pocket, and after several attempts, managed to find one to fit the lock. As he opened the door, Clay pushed him forward into the room.

The girl had been lying on the bed and now she stood against the wall, face pale and sickly in the lamplight, eyes swollen with weeping. She could not have been more than fifteen, her figure young and unformed in the shabby brown dress.

She flung herself forward wildly, making for the door, and Clay caught her by one wrist and swung her round to face him. 'Don't be afraid,' he said. 'I've come to take you home to your mother.'

She stood still and stared up into his masked face, eyes burning into his, and then her head moved slowly from side to side, as if she couldn't comprehend that this was really happening. 'Oh, God, sir, and here was I nearly going out of me mind.'

She picked up her shawl and wound it about her

head, slow, bitter tears oozing from her eyes. 'No one will harm you ever again,' Clay assured her, iron in his voice. 'You have my word on it.'

He touched her shoulder gently with one hand, and she stepped back as if she had been stung. 'For God's sake, let's go, sir, before he returns,' she said urgently.

She moved out onto the landing and Clay took the lamp from the butler and pushed him back into the room. 'He'll kill me when he gets back,' the old man said tearfully, wringing his hands.

'I shouldn't count on that,' Clay told him, and closed the door and locked it.

He tossed the keys into the shadows and followed the girl, who was already down below in the hall fumbling at the lock of the front door. When he went out into the porch, she was leaning against one of the pillars, half-fainting, and he slipped an arm about her shoulders and carried her down the steps.

All strength seemed to have deserted her and he lifted her onto Pegeen's back and swung into the saddle. As he cantered down toward the gate, she turned her head into his coat and burst into a storm of weeping.

By the time they reached the village, she had

recovered sufficiently to indicate her home. He dismounted, lifted her down to the ground and then hammered on the door with his right fist.

The girl's weeping had subsided, and as steps sounded inside, she looked up at him and said in a faint voice, 'Who are you?'

'A friend,' he said simply. 'You've got nothing to fear, my dear, now or at any time in the future.'

As the door started to open, he turned and swung lightly into the saddle and Pegeen moved quickly away out of the village and back towards Drumore.

There was a clump of trees by the Kileen side of the ford and he paused in their shadow. He did not have long to wait. Faintly on the night air came the sound of an approaching vehicle, and then a coach pulled by two horses appeared round a bend in the road and came toward him, clear in the moonlight.

The driver pulled on the reins to slow the horses as they entered the water and splashed across. They paused, heads down to drink, and Marley leaned out of the window and cried petulantly, 'For God's sake, why are we stopping, Kelly? Lay your whip across their damned hides.'

Clay urged Pegeen forward out of the trees, the

Dragoon Colt ready in his right hand. Marley had withdrawn his head and the driver was reaching for his long whip.

He was a sullen, dangerous-looking fellow with brutal features and great sloping shoulders. His mouth opened slowly in amazement as Clay paused on the other side of the ford and said cheerfully, in an Irish accent, 'A fine night for a walk, thanks be to God, and your master not needing you.'

The man started to reach under his seat and Clay raised the Colt and aimed it, the moonlight glinting on its brass frame. 'I shouldn't try it.'

The man dropped the reins and jumped down into the water. Marley leaned out of the window and said angrily, 'What's happening, Kelly? Didn't I tell you to get those damned horses moving?' In the same moment, he saw Clay and withdrew hastily into the coach.

Kelly moved out of the water no more than a yard from Pegeen's head. He made as if to pass and then turned and flung himself forward, hands reaching up to drag Clay from the saddle.

Clay pulled sharply on the reins, and as Pegeen danced away, he lifted his right boot into Kelly's face. The man staggered backwards with a groan and collapsed into the grass at the side of the road.

There was no sound from inside the coach and he moved Pegeen forward until she was standing in the shallows of the ford. 'You've got five seconds to come out of there, Marley, before I start shooting.'

There was a slight pause before the door opened and Marley scrambled down into the stream. He stood there, the ice-cold water lapping about his knees. 'I'll see you hang for this.'

He started to wade forward and Clay shook his head. 'Stay where you are. I want to talk to you.'

'Talk and be damned then,' Marley said. 'You'll get little else from me. I've no more than a sovereign in my purse.'

'I'm not interested in your money,' Clay said. 'Only in certain unpleasant aspects of your nature. I understand you consider yourself a ladies' man?'

'What the devil are you driving at?' Marley demanded, a frown on his face.

Clay shrugged. 'Apparently, the ladies have another opinion. I've got a message from Eithne Fallon. She thanks you for your hospitality, but prefers to spend the night with her mother.'

Marley's face was white in the moonlight. 'You'll pay for this.'

Clay cut him short. He pressed the muzzle of the Colt against the man's forehead. 'This is your only warning, Marley,' he said calmly. 'If I hear that you've bothered the child or her mother again, you'll get a bullet through the brain one dark night.'

'Who are you?' Marley said, and there was the beginning of fear in his voice.

Clay laughed mockingly. 'Surely you received my letter? I told you to look for me.'

Marley's jaw sagged and an expression of utter astonishment appeared on his face. 'Captain Swing!' he said in a whisper.

'Correct!' Clay told him. 'Now take off your coat.'

Marley glared up at him. 'What are you going to do?' he demanded, and there was a crack in his voice.

Clay raised the Colt threateningly without replying and Marley stripped off his expensive evening cloak and then his tailcoat. He stood shivering in his shirtsleeves, a revolting, almost pathetic figure, and Clay pointed up the road toward Kileen. 'You know where your house is. If I were you, I'd start running.'

By now Marley was thoroughly frightened. He

backed away, his mouth trembling, and then he turned and started to run towards the village.

Clay holstered his Colt and urged Pegeen toward the coach. He pulled the long horse-whip from its socket by the driver's seat and turned and cantered back to Kileen.

Marley was still twenty or thirty yards from the first cottage when he caught up with him. The whip rose and fell, the long lash settling across the man's fleshy shoulders, shredding the white cambric shirt.

Marley screamed and stumbled onto his face. Again the lash curled around his body and he staggered to his feet and lurched forward, arms raised protectingly. Clay thought of Eithne Fallon and others like her and of the things he had heard about this man, and all pity died in him. The lash rose and fell mercilessly, driving Marley toward the centre of the village.

Already lights were appearing in cottage windows and dogs barked and scratched at doors. He delivered one last vicious blow with all his strength, and as the whip curled around Marley's shoulders, the end of it sliced across his face, laying it open to the bone. He gave a dreadful cry and fell forward onto his face, unconscious.

Clay flung the whip down to the ground. As he did so, a cottage door opened and a man came forward uncertainly. Keeping a cautious eye on Clay, he dropped to one knee beside Marley's insensible body and turned him over. His breath hissed between his teeth. 'God save us all, but it's the squire.'

'When he comes round, tell him to leave young girls alone in future,' Clay said in a loud, clear voice for all to hear. 'Compliments of Captain Swing!'

In the same instant, he wheeled Pegeen sharply and urged her into a gallop. They passed Kelly, who was sitting up, head in hands, and splashed across the ford. Behind him, he could hear shouting in the village and dogs barking, but he paid no heed. Ten minutes later, he turned off the road, letting Pegeen choose her own pace as they climbed up out of the valley onto the moors.

When he reached Claremont, he rode straight into the stables and dismounted. As he unsaddled the mare, Joshua crossed the yard and Clay said, 'I'll see to the mare. You fix me a meal. I've come back with something of an appetite.'

When he entered the house a few minutes later, Joshua was busy at the stove and Clay went up to his room and unbuckled the Colt. He tossed his hat into a corner and removed the greatcoat, then he stood in front of the mirror and looked at himself.

A pulse throbbed steadily in his right temple. He ran his fingers through his hair and laughed shakily. 'That should teach the swine a lesson he'll not forget in a hurry,' he said softly.

When he went below, Joshua was laying the table. Joshua regarded him gravely and went to the cupboard and took down the brandy bottle. 'You look as if you need a drink, Colonel.'

'And perhaps another.' Clay told him.

He emptied the glass in one long swallow and coughed as its warmth flooded through him. Afterwards, he refilled it and sat by the fire and related the night's happenings as Joshua worked at the stove.

Joshua listened in silence, his face betraying no emotion. When Clay had finished, he shook his head. 'Seems to me you've done the very thing you said you wanted to avoid, Colonel. You've taken sides.'

Clay frowned. 'I can't see that – Marley was a special case.'

'But calling yourself Captain Swing was a fool thing to do. If as you say, more than one person has received threatening letters signed in that name, then the whole country will be in an uproar. Now they'll think the man really exists.'

'But he does,' Clay said. 'Or rather, he did.' He sighed. 'It was quite like old times, Josh. Riding through Indiana and Ohio with Morgan's Raiders.'

'What about that Georgian accent of yours?' Joshua persisted. 'Marley, or anyone else who heard it, won't have any difficulty in recognizing it again.'

Clay grinned. 'I was a natural mimic as a boy, you know that better than anyone. I managed a pretty fair imitation of an Irish accent back there in Kileen.'

Joshua shook his head and started to ladle food onto a plate. 'You're a naturally violent man, Colonel. That's your trouble. So was your father before you, and look how he died.'

Clay shrugged. 'At least it was quick. As a physician, I can assure you there are worse ways to go than with a bullet.'

He rose to his feet to move to the table and a horse clattered into the yard outside. A moment later, there was a knock at the door. Joshua glanced across, alarm on his face, and Clay smiled calmly and crossed the room. When he opened the door, he found Kevin Rogan standing there.

The big man smiled. 'Sorry to bother you at this hour, Colonel, but we're in need of your professional services.'

Clay motioned him in and closed the door. 'What's the trouble?'

Kevin shrugged. 'After our earlier visit to Drumore House, we went down to Cohan's pub for a drink. There was trouble with a man called Varley, one of Hamilton's boys. He cut my father up a little.'

'How bad is it?' Clay asked.

'A nasty slash on the inside of his right thigh. Varley was trying for the groin.'

'I'll get my bag,' Clay said. 'If you'll saddle Pegeen for me, it would save time.'

Rogan turned to open the door and hesitated. 'By the way, don't forget that package, Colonel. You did say you wanted to deliver it personally. Now would be as good a time as any.'

Clay nodded, a slow smile appearing on his face. 'A sound idea. It's been on my conscience for long enough.'

The door closed softly behind Rogan, and Joshua appeared from the stairs, the black bag in one hand, tweed riding coat over his left arm. As he helped

Clay into the coat, he said, 'I've taken the liberty of placing the Dragoon at the bottom of the bag, Colonel. You never can tell.'

Clay nodded thoughtfully. 'You've got a point there.'

Joshua moved across to a cupboard and took out the package. 'Presumably you'll be wanting this?'

'Perhaps I'll find out what it contains before the night's out,' Clay said. 'I think I'll make that my fee for attending Shaun Rogan.'

They went outside as Kevin emerged from the stables with Pegeen saddled and bridled, and a moment later, he and Clay clattered across the cobbles and moved up through the trees to the moors.

6

They rode in silence across the quiet moor, Kevin Rogan leading the way. As they approached the head of the valley, he gave a peculiar liquid whistle and a horseman moved out of the trees on their left, moonlight glinting on the barrel of his shotgun.

'Is it yourself, Kevin?' Dennis Rogan called softly.

'I'll send Marteen up to relieve you in an hour,' Kevin told him as they passed.

Dennis grinned cheerfully. 'Good night to ye, Colonel,' he said, and melted back into the darkness of the trees.

'So you're mounting guards now?' Clay said.

Kevin nodded. 'You might say things are beginning to warm up.' At that moment they came to the rim of the valley, and all further conversation ended as they concentrated on safely negotiating the steep path.

A dog started to bark as they rode past the paddock into the yard, and as they dismounted, the front door opened, casting a shaft of yellow light into the night.

Mrs Rogan peered out at them, a lamp in her hand as Clay walked toward her, saddlebags over one arm. 'How is he?' he asked.

She shrugged. 'He's suffered worse and lived.' She led the way along a narrow, whitewashed passage and through a door at the far end.

Clay found himself in a large, stone-flagged kitchen with rough plastered walls and ceiling and a wide fireplace. Marteen and Cathal faced each other across the table, a chessboard between them, and their father sprawled in a wing-backed chair by the fire with a deerhound at his feet.

His right trouser leg had been split open to the waist and the bandage twisted about his thigh was saturated with blood, but the blue eyes were calm in the great bearded face.

He smiled and extended a hand. 'It might be your grandfather standing there before me, God rest him.' He shook his great head and laughter echoed around the room. 'The tales I could be telling you.'

Clay warmed to the man instantly, with that instinctive liking that must come at once or not at all. As he took off his coat, he smiled. 'My grandfather seems to have cut quite a swathe through these parts as a young man.'

Shaun Rogan poured himself another whiskey. 'And that's an understatement if ever I heard one.' He chuckled. 'I can't get over how like him ye are. And just as quick off the mark. The way you stamped that gun out of Burke's hand was something to see.'

'A pity you couldn't have kicked the bastard in the face while ye were about it,' Kevin added in a hard voice.

'I considered it more important to make sure his bullet didn't go where he wanted it to.' Clay took a pair of surgical scissors from his bag and cut away the bandage from Shaun Rogan's thigh.

The wound was seven or eight inches long, with raw, angry edges. He sponged the blood away with a piece of cloth and examined it closely. After a while, he nodded in satisfaction. 'It's a clean slash. With luck, you'll be riding again in a fortnight.'

Shaun Rogan cursed fluently and Kevin grinned. 'A week or two by the fireside will do you no harm. The boys and I can manage things.'

Clay asked Mrs Rogan for some strips of linen and a basin and then he raised her husband's leg on a stool, instructing Kevin to hold it firmly in position. Next, he reached for the whiskey bottle and poured some into the open wound. Big Shaun stifled a curse and gripped the arms of his chair until the knuckles turned white, as the liquor burned into his raw flesh. 'And what the hell is that supposed to do?' he demanded.

Clay threaded a curved needle with silk. 'Bullet wounds stay clean, knife wounds tend to go bad, don't ask me why. There's a man called Lister who thinks he knows the reason, but we won't go into that now. Whiskey or any raw spirit helps to keep a wound clean. We proved that in the war.'

He started to stitch the wound and Big Shaun kept on talking, voice steady and controlled despite the great drops of cold sweat which had appeared on his forehead at the first touch of the needle. 'You were with the Confederates, weren't you, Colonel? Trust an Irishman to choose the losing side.'

'The Yankees had an Irish Brigade,' Clay said. 'At Gettysburg, their chaplain, Father Corby, gave them absolution before battle and denied Christian burial to any man who refused to fight.'

'God save us all, but he must have been the hard one,' Cathal said.

Big Shaun grunted as the needle pushed through his flesh again. 'Your father, how did he die? I knew from your uncle that he hadn't joined the army like yourself.'

'He bought two ships and made a fortune running the blockade from Nassau to Atlanta,' Clay said calmly. 'He was shot dead in a running fight with a Yankee frigate three months before the end of the war.'

Shaun Rogan solemnly crossed himself. 'May he find peace.'

'He certainly never found it this side of the grave,' Clay said.

He skilfully knotted the final stitch, snipped the loose ends, and then bandaged the leg with clean linen. As he tied the knot, Shaun Rogan sighed. 'By God, it feels better already. You know your business, Colonel.'

'I ought to, I've had enough practice,' Clay told him.

Marteen produced clean glasses and a fresh bottle of whiskey and Kevin Rogan filled a glass and pushed it across. 'The labourer is worthy of his hire, Colonel, as the good book says.'

'Ah, yes, the question of payment,' Clay said. 'I was forgetting.'

There was a slight awkward pause as the Rogans looked at each other and Big Shaun shrugged. 'Fair enough, Colonel. You've done a good job. Name your fee.'

Clay reached for his saddlebags and took out the package. 'When a man has carried something as far as I've carried this, I think he's entitled to know what's inside.'

Shaun Rogan's eyes widened in surprise and then his mouth opened and he laughed heartily. 'And by God you shall have your wish, Colonel. I think you've earned it. Open it up, Kevin.'

The package had been wrapped in canvas, sewn along the edges and sealed with red wax. Kevin produced a clasp knife and sliced open the stitches. Clay took his time over lighting one of his cheroots and waited.

There was an inner waterproof covering of oiled silk which had also been stitched into place, and when this was removed, a wooden box stood revealed. Kevin turned it upside down and packets of banknotes cascaded onto the table.

The Rogan boys grabbed for a packet each and examined them, talking excitedly. Clay turned to their father, a frown on his face. 'But I don't understand.'

Kevin tossed a packet across to him. 'Have a look at those and you soon will.'

The notes were crisp and freshly printed five dollar bills, issued in the name of the Irish Republic and signed by John Mahoney. He looked up and saw that the others were regarding him intently. 'But there is no Irish Republic.'

'There soon will be,' Kevin Rogan said harshly. 'There are thousands of members of the Brotherhood here and in America. In a few months, we will be ready to strike, and when we do, Ireland will be free again.'

'Presumably you're referring to this Fenian Brotherhood I heard so much about in Galway?'

Shaun Rogan nodded. 'This time we mean business. We want freedom and we want it now.'

'But where do the banknotes come in?'

Kevin picked one up and read from it. 'Redeemable six months after the acknowledgement of the independence of the Irish Republic.' He grinned.

'It's a neat way of raising funds, Colonel, you must agree. In return for their loans, our supporters are issued with banknotes. The money helps to free their country, and afterwards, it's returned to them.'

Clay nodded slowly. 'The man who thought of the idea had a brain, I'll grant you that.' He turned to Big Shaun. 'I was talking to Sir George Hamilton earlier this evening. He believes it to be economically impossible for Ireland to be independent, that she needs the protection of England.'

'Protection, is it?' Kevin cried bitterly. 'If what they give us is called protection, God help us when we're dead.'

His father laid a restraining hand on his arm. 'Hold your tongue. The colonel isn't aware of the facts.' He turned to Clay, eyes completely calm in the great bearded face, so that he resembled some Old Testament prophet. 'In Ireland we all live off the land, Colonel. All of us, tenant and landlord alike.'

'Having seen the living conditions of some tenants,' Clay told him, 'I can appreciate they have good cause for discontent.'

'The landowners are mostly English or Irish Protestants, which amounts to the same thing in the end,' Rogan went on. 'In the main, they depend upon rents for their income. That means a landowner has only two ways in which he can increase the return on his investment. The first is to raise the tenant's rent. The second is to try large-scale ranching of sheep or cattle.'

'Which means evicting his tenants?' Clay said.

Big Shaun nodded grimly. 'That's about the size of it, Colonel.'

'But surely there must be laws to protect people from unjust treatment?'

Kevin Rogan laughed harshly, and his father went on, 'In practice, tenants are utterly at the mercy of their landlords. They have to pay excessive rents which leave them nothing but a bare subsistence. They have to carry out improvements which in England are undertaken by the landlord, and submit to see their rents being raised because of their own improvements.'

'But there must be some legal way of fighting against such conditions,' Clay said. 'What about politics? They have their representatives in Parliament, don't they?'

'Those with a vote are coerced,' Shaun Rogan told him. 'The whole vicious system ensures the predominance of the landlord class, and men like

Hamilton and Marley can ride roughshod and terrorize the countryside with their hired bullies imported from Scotland and England.'

Out of the silence which followed, Kevin Rogan added bitterly, 'You can see now why I found Hamilton's remark about protection so ironic. England hangs on to us because she never likes to let go of anything. The system of land ownership forced on us over the centuries keeps a whole nation in poverty and causes thousands to emigrate every year.'

Clay shook his head and said soberly, 'In the face of such arguments, there's little I can say.'

'Have another drink, Colonel.' Shaun Rogan filled Clay's glass. 'To the average Englishman, the Irishman is an uncivilized ruffian, an animal who lives on potatoes. This is as great a myth as the one which suggests that all Englishmen are gentlemen. What they don't understand is that a hundred acres under potatoes will support four times as many people as a hundred acres under wheat.' He shrugged. 'But if the spuds fail, we starve.'

Clay swallowed some of his whiskey and said slowly, 'What about Sir George Hamilton? Why do you hate each other so much?'

'Because he treats us like animals – all of us. He's some kind of God and we're scum. He hates me particularly, because I own this valley and he can't touch us here.' Shaun shook his head and added in a sombre voice, 'After raising the Devil, it becomes necessary to pay him his due, as George Hamilton will find out before much longer. His hour will come.'

'Aren't you being hard on him?' Clay said. 'I understand someone tried to murder him and shot his wife by mistake. At least his bitterness and hate are understandable.'

Shaun Rogan laughed harshly. 'The best thing that ever happened to that poor woman was taking the bullet meant for him. He led her a dog's life for years. Good God, Colonel, you've seen the state his tenants are living in. Do you need further proof of the kind of man he is?'

Clay sighed heavily. 'It was foolish of me to think anything else, I suppose, but his version of his wife's death was rather different. He also told me that he and my uncle were friends.'

There was general laughter from the boys who had been following the conversation with interest. 'Friends, is it?' Kevin said. 'Your uncle slashed him across the face with his whip in the middle of the village for the whole world to see. A family had been evicted and the woman died in childbirth on the road to Galway.'

Clay's eyes narrowed, as a disturbing thought sprang into his mind. 'The fire that gutted Claremont – how did it start?'

Shaun Rogan shrugged. 'Each man has his own thoughts on that score. Your uncle lived alone with an old woman to keep house, him having fallen on hard times. There would have been nothing left at all if it hadn't been for a sudden storm of rain.'

'And you're suggesting Sir George had something to do with it?'

'I'm not suggesting anything,' Shaun Rogan said, 'except that it was a powerful coincidence.'

Clay got to his feet and walked across to the fire. He stared down into the glowing heart of it, thinking about his uncle, old and sick and alone, desperately trying to save the home that meant everything to him as flames blossomed in the night.

He threw his cheroot into the fire and turned with a grim smile. 'As you say, each man must have his own thoughts on the matter.' He moved back to the table. 'Tell me something, does your objection to Sir George extend to his niece?'

'How she ever came to be related to him, I'll never know,' Shaun said. 'You'll find no one in Drumore with anything but a good word for Miss Joanna.'

Clay picked up his glass to finish his whiskey and thought of something else. He smiled. 'Where does Cohan obtain such excellent French brandy, by the way?'

'Now how would we be knowing a thing like that, Colonel?' Kevin said.

Clay shrugged. 'Just a thought. I wondered if he had any connection with the schooner I saw unloading not three miles from here last night.'

There was a moment of complete stillness, and then Kevin roared with laughter. 'It was you, was it? I might have known. But who was your companion?'

Clay smiled. 'I'm not at liberty to say. Just a friend who enjoys a gallop by moonlight.'

'And it wouldn't take much to guess who that might be,' Big Shaun added.

Clay pulled on his coat. 'I'll drop by again tomorrow to take a look at the wound. By the way, what happened to this fellow Varley? The one who stabbed you?'

Shaun Rogan smiled softly, eyes suddenly cold

and hard. 'He made a run for it, but there are other days.'

As Clay picked up his bag, Kevin Rogan said quietly, 'Before you go, tell us one thing, Colonel. Are you with us or against us?'

Clay picked up one of the banknotes and stared at it reflectively. 'Very artistic,' he said. 'But unfortunately I've seen what an industrial nation can do in time of war to another which isn't. You'll never win. England has all the big guns.'

'Is it afraid ye are?' Marteen interrupted.

Kevin rounded on his brother fiercely. 'The Colonel is no coward. You of all people have seen sufficient proof of that.' He turned back to Clay. 'Where *do* you stand in this, Colonel? We've told you too much for comfort this night.'

'I'll not betray you, my word on that,' Clay said. 'I can't pretend to any liking for Sir George Hamilton or Marley or the rest of the breed I met at Drumore House, but I won't take sides. I've had enough trouble during the past four years to last any one man a lifetime.'

Shaun Rogan extended his right hand. 'That's good enough for me, Colonel.'

They shook hands and Clay nodded to the others and followed Kevin Rogan, who escorted him back outside. As Clay strapped his saddlebags into place and swung up into the saddle, Kevin said quietly, 'Whatever my father may say, no man can stay neutral forever, Colonel. There'll come a time when you have to choose sides, and if you don't want to make that kind of decision, you'd be better a thousand miles from Drumore.' He went back into the house and closed the door before Clay could reply.

As he followed the path toward the head of the valley, many things passed through Clay's mind. The filthy hovels owned by Sir George Hamilton in Drumore, the boy dying of consumption on his pallet against a wall streaming with water. And then there was Eithne Fallon. What would have been her fate if he hadn't brought Captain Swing to life for a few hours?

He was beginning to feel tired and his eyes were sore from lack of sleep and too much straining into the gloom. He seemed to see in the darkness an immense five dollar bill, and flames moved in from the edges devouring the words IRISH REPUBLIC and then they blossomed into great streamers that flickered toward the sky as Claremont burned.

Pegeen scrambled over the rim of the valley and Clay shook his head to bring himself back to his senses and waved a hand to Dennis Rogan, invisible in the trees. As he thundered along the track at full gallop, he knew, with a sinking heart, that already he was having to choose sides, despite himself.

7

The day was exhilarating and the blue sky dipped away to the horizon, but as Clay rode out of the courtyard and took the path which led up through the trees, his face was grave and sombre.

Earlier that morning, he had gone down to the village to visit the boy with consumption and had arrived to find Father Costello administering the last rites. Despite everything Clay had done to make the child's last moments on earth easier, he had hung on to life tenaciously for another hour and his ending had not been pleasant to see.

The moor was purple with heather and Clay reined in beside a black tarn where bog-lilies floated and the wind whispered through dry whins. A plover cried plaintively as it lifted across the lower slopes of the hill, and then there was silence, and a strange sadness fell upon him at the thought of the young life ended before it had really begun.

He touched spurs lightly to Pegeen, taking her away from that quiet place and galloped toward the sea. The haze of the fall was over the land and the wind that moved in from the Atlantic to meet him was warm. He dismounted, and leaving Pegeen to crop the long grass, sat by the edge of the cliffs and stared out to sea. It was there that Joanna Hamilton found him half an hour later.

She slid from the saddle before he could rise and moved toward him, her face solemn. 'I called at Claremont and Joshua told me about the boy. I'm sorry.'

He shrugged. 'Don't be. I've seen so much of death on the grand scale during the past four years that another one more or less doesn't seem to make a great deal of difference.'

'But this one was so unnecessary,' she said fiercely. 'We both know that. If these people were given decent homes to live in instead of being treated like animals, this sort of thing wouldn't happen.'

'I wouldn't advise you to keep to that line of argument,' he said, 'unless you want me to visit your uncle for the express purpose of putting a bullet through him. That's exactly how I felt when I stood by that child's bed.'

There was a slight pause and she made an obvious effort to change the subject. 'Did you hear what happened in Kileen last night?'

Clay shook his head and said calmly, 'No, should I have?'

'The whole of Drumore is buzzing with it. Hugh Marley of Kileen House was waylaid on his way home from our reception last night and flogged in the main street of Kileen with most of his tenants looking on.'

She filled in the details with remarkable accuracy, and when she had finished, Clay smiled. 'I can't say my heart bleeds for him. From what I heard last night, he deserves everything he got.'

'That seems to be the general opinion,' she said. 'The mysterious Captain Swing has become a hero overnight.'

'Have you any idea who he might be?'

She shook her head. 'I had thought of Kevin Rogan, but it could be anyone.'

'And what does your uncle think about all this?'

'He's sent a letter by special messenger to Galway asking for the cavalry to turn out, but they've got better ways of spending their time than scouring the country looking for one man, especially with the country in the state it is.'

'It all seems so melodramatic,' Clay said. 'What could he ever hope to achieve on his own, this Captain Swing of yours? To ride masked through the countryside by night and waving a pistol is all very fine, but how much can it help the present situation?'

She flushed and there was an edge of anger in her voice. 'He's already brought hope back to people who'd forgotten the meaning of the word. For that, at least, we should be grateful to him. Surely you can see that?'

'I'll give you the same sort of answer I gave Shaun Rogan last night,' Clay replied. 'Having just spent four years at close quarters with melodrama on the grand scale, you'll appreciate that lost causes now have little appeal for me.'

She looked surprised. 'How did you come to meet Shaun Rogan?'

He told her what had happened, and when he had finished, she bit her lip in vexation. 'I knew nothing of this trouble at Cohan's last night. Now things will be even worse between my uncle and the Rogans. What did you think of them?'

Clay shrugged. 'I liked them. The boys are a trifle wild, but they'll turn into fine men if they live that long.'

'Meaning you think they'll all come to a bad end?' she asked.

'A rope's end,' Clay told her, 'unless they change their ways and abandon this wild scheme of taking part in a rebellion against England. It's doomed to failure.'

'But they've got right on their side,' she insisted.

'Might is right,' he said. 'The English invented that saying, and have spent a great deal of time and effort proving it in practice.'

For a little while, she sat with a slight frown on her face, and then she said slowly, 'I want to understand you, Clay, but I know so little about you. Why did you really come to Drumore?'

'I wanted to see Claremont. It was as simple as that.'

'But what's left of it is of no great value,' she persisted. 'If it was money you were hoping for, you've had a wasted journey. Even to my uncle it isn't worth a great deal.'

He lay back in the grass, hands locked behind his head. 'Money is the least of my worries. My father bought ships and made a fortune running the Yankee blockade from Nassau to Atlanta. He was killed just before the end of the war. He left me a million pounds sterling on deposit in the Bank of England.'

She gasped. 'I feel like a pauper by comparison,' she said, with a light laugh. 'He must have been a remarkable man.'

'Some men swore he had the Devil in him,' Clay said. 'He was the most dangerous man I've ever known. My mother was a gentle, lovely creature, the only person who could ever control him. She was never very strong. She died when I was ten.'

For a moment, he brooded quietly, alone with the past. 'After that, he sold the plantation and we moved away. Things had been going from bad to worse for some time. He wasn't a notable success as a cotton planter. We never stayed anywhere for long. He was a natural gambler, and for several years he worked the Mississippi riverboats, earning a living at it. Later, he went to Virginia City and opened a saloon.'

'And what did you do?' Joanna asked.

'Hung on to his coat tails,' Clay told her. 'I had a remarkable education, believe me. I first saw him shoot a man dead when I was twelve. After that, we never looked back, but all good things have to come to an end. He decided it was time I had some formal schooling, and I went back East to live with my mother's brother in New York. When I was eighteen, my father discovered my interest in medicine and sent me to London and Paris to complete my studies. He never did anything by halves.'

'And then came the war?'

'Not quite. He sold out in Virginia City and returned to Georgia, bought a great plantation and tried to live like a gentleman again. It was too late, of course. He'd been living by the twin senses of action and passion for too long. But passion is no substitute for love. Love grows, passion consumes. He was mixed up in one damned scandal after another. Other men's wives – the usual things. The war came just in time to save him from drinking himself into the ground.'

'And yet he didn't join the army?'

Clay nodded. 'No, he left that to fools like me, as he said on the day I left to join my regiment.'

'You'd been living with him then?'

'For two years after I got back from Paris,' Clay told her.

'Didn't your father agree with the South's reasons for going to war?' she said.

Clay shook his head. 'It wasn't that – he knew we couldn't win, that's all.'

'Then why did *you* fight?' she asked simply.

He frowned. 'I don't really know. There were so many reasons. Because I was born in Georgia. Because my friends and neighbours were going to war. Isn't that really the only reason any man ever fights?'

'And so you rode off to your lost cause after all.'

'In the beginning, it was anything but that,' he said. 'It was gallant men and horses, bugles faintly on the wind – all the mystique of soldiering. In the early days, it wasn't too far to Richmond, pretty women in ball gowns and handsome men in magnificent uniforms.'

'And afterwards?' she demanded.

He smiled grimly. 'Afterwards, it was the Yankee blockade and slow starvation. I thought we were going to pull it off in July '64, when Jubal Early erupted from the Shenandoah Valley and frightened 'em to death in Washington, but it was too late. I can't begin to describe the kind of hell those last nine months were.'

'One thing still puzzles me,' she said. 'You started out as an army surgeon and ended as commander of a brigade of cavalry. How did that happen?'

'The fortunes of war,' he replied. 'In the summer of '63, I was on detachment with General Morgan when he made his famous raid into Kentucky, Indiana and Idaho. We were captured and the Yankees, not taking kindly to raiders, refused to treat us as prisoners of war. I was included with the other officers, surgeon or not. We were all imprisoned in the Illinois State Penitentiary.'

'But that was infamous,' she said indignantly. 'You were only obeying orders.'

'It didn't really matter, we'd no intention of staying.' He chuckled deeply in his throat. 'We stole table knives from the dining hall, dug through two feet of concrete floor and tunnelled under the prison yard to the outer wall. Naturally, we left the governor a polite note telling him how much we'd appreciated his hospitality.'

'Did you have much trouble in reaching the Confederate lines?' she asked.

He shook his head. 'Not really – one of the few advantages of a civil war. It's so difficult to know your enemy when he's out of uniform. When I rejoined the army, I asked to became an active cavalry officer. The Yankees had me on their list and obviously would not treat me as a non-combatant in the future, so I didn't really have much choice.'

'It seems you had a talent for it,' she said, with a slight smile.

'Mostly it consisted of trying to stay alive. And of taking only calculated risks. Not like Morgan. He took the pitcher to the well once too often and raided into Tennessee. His command was cut to ribbons at a place called Granville. They caught him hiding behind some vines in a garden and shot him through the heart.'

He wrinkled his brow and narrowed his eyes, trying to pierce the limitless depths of the sky, as he thought of Morgan and his father, so much alike in their attitude to life. She sat quietly beside him and said nothing.

She stared out to sea, immersed in her own thoughts. He gazed at her dispassionately and it was as if he had never really seen her before. How could he possibly have thought her not beautiful? She was lovely, with the wind bringing the stain of roses to her cheeks, and the dark depths of her eyes were places a man might drown in willingly.

She turned and discovered him looking at her,

flushed and said hurriedly, 'And what do you intend to do when you leave Drumore?'

He shrugged. 'There's no rush, I want to get the stink of war out of my nostrils. I came here to find a little peace, but already forces beyond my control are pulling me in several directions. Whatever happens, I'll never return to Georgia. I've been considering California. Now there's a fine country for you.'

He closed his eyes and she said slowly, 'Sometimes we have to stand and meet the problem that faces us here and now, Clay. No man is an island. Isn't that what a poet once said? I think in a way, that your father tried to live amongst other people and yet apart from them, and found in the end that it wouldn't work.'

He sighed. It was only to be expected that she would think that way, that the problems of these people would be her problems. She was young and she was lovely and had a kind heart. Somewhere a lark sang high in the sky, but it only touched the edge of his consciousness. Her voice moved on and then began to rise and fall and finally became the timeless, sad sough of the sea.

* * *

He awakened suddenly. Above him, clouds turned and wheeled across the sky and hinted at a break in the weather. She had disappeared. For a moment, a strange irrational panic caused him to rush to the edge of the cliff and then he saw her down on the beach at the water's edge. A crazily tilted path fell away beneath him and he began a careful descent.

She was standing knee-deep in the sea, and held the skirt of her riding habit bunched in one hand while she splashed in the water with the other like a small child. His boots grated upon the shingle and she turned at once and waded toward him.

'You deserted me,' he said. 'I awakened to find you gone, like some enchanted princess in a fairy tale.'

'After you fell asleep, I came down to the beach. The water looked so inviting I couldn't resist it,' she said.

Her boots and stockings stood on a boulder at the foot of the path. She started toward them and gave a slight exclamation as she stepped on a jagged stone. Clay swung her up into his arms without a word and carried her quickly across the shingle.

When he reached the boulder, he stood for a

moment holding her, gazing down into her eyes, her warmth and softness quickening the blood in his veins, and after a while, she turned her face into his chest.

He set her down and said awkwardly, 'I'll go back and see to the horses. Can you manage the path on your own?'

She nodded, averting her eyes. 'I'll only be five minutes.'

When he reached the top of the path, his hands were still trembling. He lit a cheroot with some difficulty because of the wind, and then collected both horses and led them back toward the clifftop. As he did so, she appeared over the edge.

She moved through the long, dry grass and the sun was behind her. He crinkled his eyes and her image blurred at the edges until, when she paused for a moment and looked out to sea again, she might have been a painting by one of the great masters. She looked unreal and ethereal and completely and utterly beautiful.

He dropped the reins and moved toward her, and this time there was nothing of fear in her eyes, only a great warmth, and she came to meet him, a steady, grave smile touching her lips.

She held out her hands, and as he took them,

there was a sudden cry in the distance and the sound of hooves drumming on the turf. He turned quickly and saw Joshua approaching at the gallop mounted on the coach horse.

He reined in and wiped sweat from his brow with a large handkerchief. 'I'm sure glad I found you, Colonel. Father Costello sent a message up to the house. Says there's a woman called Cooney having a child in Drumore and she needs you bad.'

Joanna was already moving to her mount and Clay quickly lifted her into the saddle. As he turned to Pegeen, Joshua handed him his saddlebags. 'Everything you need in there, Colonel,' he said. 'You make tracks. I'll never keep up with you on this horse.'

'You stay at the house,' Clay said. 'If I need you, I'll send a message.' Already Joanna was away, galloping across the moor, and he put spurs to Pegeen and thundered after her.

8

Clouds moved over the face of the sun and a great belt of shadow spilled darkness like a fast-spreading stain across the ground. As they entered the village, rain started to fall and ragged, barefooted children ran after their horses, hands outstretched for the odd coin. Clay tossed a handful of loose change to scatter them, and he and Joanna moved on past Cohan's and reined in outside the Cooneys' cottage.

As they dismounted, the door opened, and Father Costello emerged, relief on his face. 'I'm glad you've come,' he said. 'She's having a hard time of it, poor soul.'

Joanna moved past him into the cottage as Clay started to unstrap his saddlebags. 'Is her husband here?'

Father Costello shook his head. 'He left for Galway yesterday and hasn't returned yet. He was hoping to borrow money from a brother of his in trade. He's a month behind with his rent and Sir George threatened to evict him if the arrears were not paid by Monday.'

Clay frowned. 'That was three days ago.'

'Exactly!' the priest said. 'I'm hoping Sir George is exercising a little Christian charity for once, knowing of the circumstances. He owes them some consideration. Michael Cooney was in his employ for nine years until Burke dismissed him for long absences due to bad health.'

'Charity is the last virtue I can imagine Sir George practising,' Clay said.

The old priest sighed. 'I must agree with you, but the world is full of surprises. However, I mustn't keep you from your patient. I'm going up the street to the Flahertys' to see to their son's funeral arrangements. I'll look in later, if I may.' He walked away, the skirts of his robe lifted against the mud and Clay went into the cottage.

The old crone still huddled by the turf fire, mumbling to herself, and Joanna was in the act of lighting an oil lamp which stood upon the table. She nodded toward the bed without speaking and Clay put down his saddlebags and crossed the room.

Mrs Cooney was only half-conscious, her face twisted with pain. He quickly loosened her clothing and examined her, his hands moving gently across the swollen belly. After a moment, he straightened and walked back to the table.

'Get me a cup of water,' he said to Joanna, and opened his bag. When she brought the water, he mixed an opiate and, returning to Mrs Cooney, gently forced open her mouth. She coughed so that a trickle of moisture oozed from one corner, but after a while her head eased back against the pillow and she began to breathe deeply.

Clay moved back to the table with the empty cup, face grave. 'Who's been attending to her previously?'

Joanna nodded toward the woman by the fire. 'Old Mrs Byrne there is the village midwife. She's tried everything, but the child refuses to come.'

'I'm not surprised,' Clay said. 'It isn't in the correct position for a natural delivery.'

'Why not?' she said.

He shrugged. 'Many reasons. She's probably been working too hard for one thing, but it's immaterial now.' He started to take off his coat. 'You'll have to help me. Strip her quickly and get her onto the cleanest sheet you can find. We've no time for modesty.'

'Are you going to operate?' Joanna said. 'What do they call it – a Cesarean?'

He laughed grimly. 'Not a chance – especially under these conditions. The mother always dies and the child usually does. It's only a form of homicidal witchcraft.'

He rolled up his sleeves and poured whiskey over his hands. He dried them on a clean cloth as he watched Joanna and the old crone make the woman ready.

By now she was completely under the influence of the opiate, and after they had stripped her naked, she lay in the dim light of the oil lamp, breathing heavily. They drew up her knees and he made a further examination.

'What do you think?' Joanna said.

'It isn't going to be quite as difficult as I first thought.'

He took a pair of forceps from his instrument bag and went and knelt on the end of the bed. It took him several patient minutes to secure the head of the child, but finally he gave a grunt of satisfaction and locked the two handles together.

At that moment, the door of the cottage burst open and someone entered the room. Clay glanced quickly over his shoulder. Peter Burke stood there with two of his Scotsmen and they were carrying shotguns.

Clay turned back to his task and said evenly, 'Tell them to get out, Joanna.'

Joanna straightened up, her face white and angry, and Burke said, 'No use, Miss Hamilton. We've got strict instructions from your uncle. The Cooneys must go. They've had their chance.'

'You wouldn't treat a dog like this,' she exploded. 'Do you expect the child to be delivered in the middle of the street or in Cohan's bar parlour, perhaps?'

He shrugged. 'The colonel can have time to deliver the child, but after that Mrs Cooney must go. Someone will take her in, no doubt.'

Clay wiped sweat from his brow with one hand and said to Joanna, 'Pass my bag, will you?'

She placed it on the end of the bed, and he smiled. 'I think you'll find a pistol in the bottom somewhere.'

Her hand emerged from the bag clutching the

heavy Dragoon Colt, and the lamplight glinted on its brass frame. 'All you do is thumb back the hammer and pull the trigger,' Clay said. 'I'll be happy to extract the bullet from Mr Burke after I've finished here.'

Joanna moved past him, the Colt held in both hands, its barrel trained on the exact centre of Burke's waistcoat. 'I'll give you five seconds to get out of here,' she said coldly.

'I should do as she says if I were you, Burke,' Clay added. 'That gun has a hair trigger.'

The two Scotsmen gave ground at once, but for a moment Burke hesitated, glaring at Joanna. She thumbed back the hammer, and as the deliberate metallic click echoed through the stillness, he turned with an oath and the door banged behind him.

Joanna moved quickly and bolted it and then she went back to the bed and replaced the Colt in the bag. 'Hold her knees,' Clay said. 'In spite of the opiate, she may feel some pain. Whatever happens, keep her still.'

He took a deep breath, made sure the handles of the forceps were securely locked, and pulled down. The child began to move. He straightened the forceps and then started to pull steadily upwards, and miraculously, the child was there on the sheet at the end of the bed.

Clay dropped the forceps and examined it carefully. Except for the slight and temporary indentations where the head had been gripped, it seemed healthy and unharmed, a fine boy, and he quickly double-knotted the cord and then severed it with a scalpel.

He lifted the child up and handed him across to the old crone as Joanna, with that inborn knowledge granted to all women, gently and expertly helped the mother and cleansed the blood from her body.

Clay stood watching her for a moment. 'Obviously, this wasn't your first time.'

Joanna looked up and shook her head. 'I'm often called out to help. Will she be all right now?'

He nodded. 'I think so. There's always child-bed fever, but they seem to catch that much more readily in hospital than they do at a home confinement.'

'You certainly seemed to know what you were doing,' she said.

He grinned. 'This wasn't *my* first time, either.'

He was sweating and he lifted the whiskey bottle

to his lips and took a long swallow. Then she was at his shoulder and crying, her arms about him, head against his chest. No words needed to be said.

He held her close, one hand gently stroking her hair, no particular feeling of joy sweeping through him, because he had known that this would happen from that first meeting – they had both known.

For a little while longer, he held her, and then he gently pushed her away, unbarred the door and stepped outside. Burke and his men were waiting for him, drawn up in a line ten yards distant from the cottage, their shotguns ready.

Several men were standing outside the pub, waiting to see what would happen, Cohan at the front of them in a soiled apron, and women hurried through the rain to chase children indoors out of harm's way.

For a short while, no one spoke. The only sound was the quiet hiss of the rain as it splashed into the mud, and then Burke moved forward, his two men keeping pace with him.

He was obviously controlling himself with difficulty. 'If you've finished your business in there, I'll carry out my orders, Colonel.'

'Tell me something,' Clay said calmly. 'How much do the Cooneys owe?'

A wary expression appeared at once on Burke's face. 'I can't see how that concerns you.'

'But it does,' Clay said. 'And more than you know. I intend to pay those arrears personally to Sir George this afternoon.'

Burke shook his head stubbornly. 'That's nothing to do with me. I have my orders and I intend to carry them out.'

Clay took one quick pace forward, and hit him in the mouth so hard that he skinned his knuckles, and Burke, caught off balance, staggered backwards into the mud.

The two Scotsmen dropped their shotguns and moved in on Clay and he backed against the wall. His opponents, with their hard, brutal features, would obviously draw a thin line between a beating and a killing. From the look of them, once they got him down, they would finish the job with their heavy boots.

As Burke rose to his feet and moved in behind them, help came from an unexpected quarter. A shotgun echoed flatly through the rain, and they all turned to see Kevin Rogan sitting his horse a few feet away.

One of the Scotsmen made a move toward his weapon, and Kevin said, 'I've another barrel here.' There was a hard smile on his face. 'There's nothing I like better than a good fight, but the odds are a little long at three to one.'

'You needn't have butted in, Rogan,' Burke told him. 'I'd no intention of allowing my men to spoil my pleasure.' He motioned them away quickly and turned to face Clay. 'I'll be happy to accommodate you, Colonel,' he said, and started to take off his coat.

He stripped well, great muscles rippling under his shirt and he looked completely sure of himself as he came forward. Clay had last fought with his fists as a boy of fifteen. Now, by some strange quirk of memory, the scene came back to him vividly. A wharf at Natchez on a hot July afternoon, casks booming hollowly as men unloaded a riverboat, and the circle of unfriendly faces as his opponent moved in on him.

He had lost that fight, lost it badly, which was a poor omen. He launched himself forward and Burke took a pace backwards, handed him off with a stiff right arm and whipped his left across savagely.

Clay lay in the mud for a moment, his head

singing from the force of the blow. Somewhere there was a cry, and as he started to get to his feet, Joanna appeared beside him. 'He'll kill you, Clay,' she said desperately. 'He blinded a tinker in a prizefight at Galway Fair three months ago.'

Clay pushed her away and moved forward again. Burke's teeth gleamed as he smiled. 'You don't look too good, Colonel,' he said. 'But there's more to come – much more.'

He feinted with his right, drawing Clay's guard, and delivered a powerful blow to his stomach. As Clay started to heel over, Burke hit him again, high on the right cheek, splitting the flesh to the bone and sending him backwards into the mud.

Somewhere a woman screamed, and a child started to cry, but otherwise there was silence as the village waited for the end. Through the mist, a small inner voice kept telling him what a fool he had been. So Burke was heavier by thirty pounds and an expert with his fists? There were other ways. In life, as in war, it was the quick, the unexpected that won the day. Without it, a man had to eat dirt.

Clay stayed down until his head cleared a little, watching Burke's boots cautiously as the other waited. When he moved, he came up from the ground and launched himself forward. He ducked under Burke's arm, twisted a shoulder inwards and sent him over his hip in a cross-buttock that drove the wind from the man's body.

It was then that Burke made his mistake. Half-stunned and shocked though he was by that terrible throw, he tried to get up at once. As he rose to one knee, Clay moved in fast and delivered two fierce blows to the man's unprotected face with all his force. Burke's head snapped back and he rolled over and lay still.

A ragged cheer echoed through the rain, and as Clay turned, the villagers swarmed around him, hands thumping him on the back, admiring grins on every side.

Clay was winded and sick and he couldn't remember clearly what it was all about. One thing was certain. He had been lucky – incredibly lucky. Burke's fists were lethal weapons. He had not been defeated by superior skill, but by the twin elements of surprise and one deadly wrestling trick taught to a young boy by an old Indian fighter many years before.

The crowd parted and Kevin Rogan appeared, grinning hugely. 'My father will curse the day he missed this, Colonel.' Clay sagged a little and the big man slipped an arm about his shoulder, concern on his face. 'Easy now, you'd best sit down for a while.'

They went into the cottage and Joanna pulled a chair forward. As Clay slumped into it, Kevin poured a generous measure of whiskey into a cup. 'Drink this, Colonel,' he said. 'There are few men who can say they've been in a fit state to do the same after fighting with Peter Burke.'

Joanna's face was white and anxious. 'Your face,' she said in horror. 'The flesh is split to the bone. I thought he was going to kill you.'

'He very nearly did,' Clay assured her. He got to his feet and Kevin helped him on with his coat.

'Are you sure you'll be all right?' Joanna said.

Clay nodded. 'I'll go back to Claremont and get into a hot tub. I'll survive.'

'I'll ride with him, Miss Hamilton,' Kevin said. 'I'm going home anyway.'

She smiled gratefully. 'I'd feel easier in my mind.' She smiled up at Clay and smoothed his lapels in a small, intimate gesture. 'I'll stay with Mrs Cooney for a while. I don't think there will be any more trouble. I'll try to see you later on.'

He nodded and went outside. Burke was sitting against the wall, groaning slightly, as one of his men slapped him in the face, and Clay mounted Pegeen and rode through the crowd followed by Kevin Rogan.

He was still suffering from the effects of those first few terrible blows, and when they were two or three hundred yards outside the village and screened by trees, he stopped and was violently sick.

After a moment, he looked up with a tired grin. 'I feel much better for that.'

'All you need is a lie-down, Colonel,' Kevin assured him.

'Later perhaps,' Clay said. 'But not now. I've got a call to make first. It's time I told Sir George Hamilton exactly what I thought of him.'

'You might do better to sleep it off,' Kevin Rogan said warningly.

Clay shook his head. 'No, I prefer to go when I'm in the mood. Besides, there's the matter of the Cooneys' rent to take care of. I intend to pay their arrears.'

'But it isn't the money he's after, Colonel,' Kevin Rogan said. 'It's their land and cottage he wants for some purpose of his own, otherwise he'd have allowed them to go on, month after month, binding themselves to him body and soul.'

'He'll take the money if I have to ram it down his throat,' Clay said grimly.

Kevin Rogan sighed. 'I can see you're set on it, Colonel. I wish I could come with you, but it's essential I get home as soon as possible. I've important business on tonight.'

Clay leaned across and shook hands with him. 'You've helped me enough for one day. Tell your father I'll drop by tomorrow morning to have a look at that thigh of his.' He turned Pegeen off the road and up through the trees before the other could reply.

Once on top of the moor, he broke into a gallop and the wind began to revive him. He skirted the village and entered the grounds of Drumore House through a gap in the wall near the stables and cantered round to the front.

The old butler who opened the door was too well trained to show any surprise at the condition of Clay's face. He asked him to wait a moment and disappeared. After a little while, he returned and led the way along the passage to the conservatory. This time, however, he opened a door on the right and showed Clay into a small comfortably furnished study. 'Sir George will be with you in a little while, Colonel,' he said. 'May I get you a drink?'

Clay shook his head and the butler withdrew. Clay sat down in a wing-backed chair by the door and closed his eyes. The door had been left slightly ajar and he became aware of voices. Steps approached, and as they stopped outside, the butler said, 'Now mind your manners when Sir George speaks to you, my man.'

Clay turned his head and peered through the crack. A small, rat-faced man in a shabby tweed suit stood humbly, hat in hands, as the butler opened the door into the conservatory for him. As they disappeared inside, Clay leaned back, a frown on his face. Somewhere, he had seen the man before. He had a memory for faces and this was one not easily forgotten – and then he remembered. That first night in Cohan's bar. The little man had been one of those listening to Dennis boast of the holdup on the Galway Road.

There was something strange here, surely. Clay peered out through the crack again in time to see the butler return on his own and disappear in the direction of the buttery. For a moment, Clay hesitated, and then he stepped across the passage and gently opened the opposite door.

The moist heat of the conservatory enveloped him as he moved inside and he could hear voices. He turned to the left and tiptoed along a smaller path which ran parallel to the main one. A moment later, he was cautiously viewing Sir George Hamilton and his visitor from behind a screen of vines.

'Get on with it, O'Brian,' Sir George said. 'What have you managed to find out?'

'Oh, something good, your honour. Something special,' O'Brian told him.

'It had better be. God knows I'm paying you enough,' Sir George said acidly.

'It'll do ye no good to try and keep a watch on the Rogans, because they've got guards out on the approaches to Hidden Valley,' O'Brian said. 'But just before midnight, they're picking up a cargo from a Galway fishing boat. What it is, I don't know, but something special. Arms, I think.'

'It would be difficult to catch them at it,' Sir George mused. 'Their sentries would see us crossing that last half-mile of moor to the cliffs. If the cargo is as important as you say, they'll take extra care.'

'I've thought of that, your honour,' O'Brian said. 'They've arranged to carry the stuff by pony to Drumore Woods and transfer it to carts there.'

Sir George gave an exclamation of triumph. 'By God, what a place for an ambush. There's only one path through the woods. We can box them in.' He turned away, eyes glittering, fingers interlacing nervously. 'This will be a hanging offence. A hanging offence.' He tugged on a cord which disappeared through the foliage above his head, and somewhere in the distance, Clay heard a bell ring.

He moved back along the path. A moment later, the door opened and the butler came in. Clay waited until he had joined Sir George and the informer, and then he opened the door and stepped out into the passage. It was quiet and deserted and he returned to the study and closed the door.

A few minutes later, Sir George came in. The smile faded from his lips as he saw the condition of Clay's face. 'God bless my soul, Colonel, what's happened?'

Clay smiled calmly. 'I've just given your man Burke the thrashing of his life.'

Sir George frowned. 'You'd oblige me by stating the facts.'

'Gladly!' Clay told him. 'I was attending the confinement of a Mrs Cooney, a tenant of yours, I understand. Burke marched in with two armed men at the most critical moment of the delivery and announced that he had come to evict the family for non-payment of rent. Did you give him the order?'

'Naturally, Colonel,' Sir George said tranquilly. 'This is, after all, my property.' He shook his head. 'If Burke was insolent I shall punish him, for he must learn to keep his place, but don't waste your sympathy on such wretched creatures as the Cooneys. The husband is a lying, idle vagabond who never did a decent day's work in his life. That's why I had him dismissed.'

'And what happens to the wife?' Clay demanded. 'Not to mention the child. If I'm informed correctly, this wouldn't be the first time you forced a family out in such circumstances. Wasn't there a woman who died in a ditch on the road to Galway, giving birth to her child? I believe my uncle and you had a difference of opinion on the matter.'

'By God, sir, you go too far!' Sir George said, his face darkening.

'We've wasted enough time in talk,' Clay told him. 'I've come to pay the arrears in rent, plus what is due for another six months. It should at least assure the poor wretches a breathing space.'

'But I don't want your money, Colonel Fitzgerald,'

Sir George told him coldly. 'I want what is due to me to come from the Cooneys – no one else.'

Clay frowned in puzzlement for a moment, and then, recalling Kevin Rogan's words, a great light dawned. It was as if he had never seen the man before. 'Why, you actually *want* to see those poor devils out on the road. That's what you really want – not the money.'

Sir George Hamilton's face turned purple and his eyes glittered. 'After what they did to my wife, Colonel, I feel I am entitled to treat these savages in any way I choose.'

Clay laughed harshly. 'The bullet which was meant for you carried sweet release for your wife, Hamilton. You gave her hell on earth for years. You don't hate those poor devils because of her – it's that loathsome, filthy thing which flowers in your body and the taste of it in your mouth that you hate. You're frightened, my friend – frightened to die, and there isn't one single, solitary soul who'll stand at your graveside and do anything but spit.'

Sir George opened his mouth to speak, but then seemed to choke, and clawed at his stiff white collar with one hand. He tore it away convulsively and lurched to the sink. Clay stood and listened to him choking for a moment, with no pity in his heart, and then turned and walked away.

He was tired when he rode into the courtyard at Claremont, more tired than he had been in a long time. A horse was tethered by the door, and as he dismounted, Joanna emerged, followed by Joshua. 'Where have you been? I've been worried to death.'

'Having a word with your uncle,' he told her, as he went into the kitchen. 'I'm afraid we won't be on speaking terms from now on.'

He swayed slightly and caught hold of the edge of the table, and Joshua steadied him with one hand and gently led him across to the stair door. 'It's bed for you, Colonel,' he said, concern in his voice. 'You've had quite a day.'

They mounted the stairs, Joanna following, and went into his bedroom. As Joshua peeled the coat from his master's tired body, Clay examined his face in the mirror, but suddenly a mist seemed to form there and then his vision blurred and he fell across the bed.

Joanna cried out in alarm, 'Oh, God, he's hurt,' and leaned anxiously across him.

Joshua lifted his master's legs up onto the bed and pulled off his boots. 'I've seen him do this before, Miss Hamilton. Keel over after a period of intense stress. The colonel's like a thoroughbred – kind of highly strung.'

'As if I need to be told that,' she said, and Clay smiled and allowed the darkness to flow over him.

He awakened to night and moonlight streaming in through the window with ghostly fingers. For a little while, he lay there, something nagging away at the back of his mind, and then he remembered and threw back the bedclothes.

The lamp stood on the dresser and he found a match and lit it. There was a dull ache somewhere behind his eyes, his ribs were sore and there was no feeling at all in his left cheek, the one Burke had split to the bone. He touched it gingerly with a finger and winced. There was a purple patch in the pit of his stomach, blue bruises in various other places and a graze on his chin.

As he examined them, they all began to hurt and he grinned and started to dress. The immediate problem was to warn the Rogans of the intended ambush, but how? If he simply rode across to Hidden Valley and told them in person or sent Joshua with a message, it would be taken as a declaration of allegiance – an open one at that. No, it would never do. He stamped on the floor hard with his booted foot and pulled his shirt over his head.

After a moment, the door opened and Joshua entered. He said patiently, 'Now Colonel, you should be in bed.'

'Has Miss Hamilton gone? What time is it?'

Joshua consulted his watch. 'A little after nine.'

'Then I haven't got much time. I know this will distress you, Joshua, but I'm afraid Captain Swing must ride again.'

He opened the trunk and took out his cavalry greatcoat and explained the situation hurriedly as he dressed. 'And you think one of the Rogan boys will still be on guard where you saw the other one?' Joshua asked, when he had finished.

Clay knotted the scarf about his neck and pulled the brim of the hat down over his eyes. 'I certainly hope so. If not, I'll have to think of something else.'

They went downstairs and saddled Pegeen between them, and a moment later, he moved out of the yard into the dark shadows of the trees.

The moors were quiet and deserted, the only sound the lonely sighing of the wind through the heather, and clouds obscured the moon. When he was near to Hidden Valley, he turned off the track and approached from another direction, Pegeen's hooves quiet on the damp turf.

He left her tethered to a bush in a small valley by a runnel of water and climbed up its side, entering the clump of trees in which Dennis Rogan had been hiding. He went forward cautiously and after a moment heard a slight cough, and the wind carried with it the rich animal smell of a horse.

Clay paused behind a beech tree and drew his Colt. As he did so, clouds moved and a shaft of moonlight pierced the trees and fell upon the face of Marteen Rogan, who was sitting on a fallen log, a horse tethered beside him.

The horse raised its head and whinnied a warning. Clay stepped forward, Colt raised threateningly as Marteen turned. The boy's jaw went slack. 'Jesus help us, it's Captain Swing,' he said in a whisper.

'Right first time, Marteen,' Clay said lightly, in

an Irish accent. 'Now turn your back like a good lad and no harm will come to you.'

The boy did as he was told and raised his hands. 'God save us, Captain, but aren't we on the same side?'

'In a manner of speaking,' Clay told him. 'But I've no time for idle chatter. Your brother Kevin and his friends have a rendezvous in Drumore Woods, I understand. Tell him Sir George Hamilton and his men intend to be there. Tell him also to be careful how he opens his mouth in future in the hearing of a small man called O'Brian who frequents Cohan's pub.'

The boy seemed bereft of speech and Clay pushed him toward his horse. 'Up with you, lad. You'll have to ride fast if you want to foil Sir George.'

'God bless ye, Captain,' Marteen said, and swung into the saddle. A moment later, he moved out of the trees and galloped away into the night.

Clay holstered his Colt and returned to Pegeen. He climbed wearily into the saddle and started back toward Claremont. All at once, he was tired again. It had been a long day, but at least it had ended satisfactorily.

Joshua was waiting anxiously. Clay dismounted

and, leaving Joshua to unsaddle Pegeen, went up to his bedroom and undressed. He got into bed and lay staring up at the ceiling. After a while, Joshua came up with a hot toddy and refused to go until the last drop had been drunk.

After Joshua had blown out the lamp and departed, Clay lay staring up at the shadows on the ceiling, thinking about Drumore Woods and wondering what was happening there at that very moment.

It was only long afterwards that he heard how Burke and his men had waited in the woods through the cold night until, when the first grey light of dawn seeped through the trees, Burke sent a man to scout the path, who returned with a piece of paper he had found pinned to a tree at the edge of the wood.

It carried the simple message COMPLIMENTS OF CAPTAIN SWING, written in Cathal Rogan's neat, scholarly hand, but what Burke said when he read it, or Sir George, was not recorded.

9

Clay awakened from a deep, dreamless sleep. His face was stiff and there was a dull ache in the pit of his stomach, but otherwise he felt fine. Whatever Joshua had put in the toddy had certainly done the trick.

He sat on the edge of the bed and reached for his hunter, seeing with surprise that it was almost three o'clock. He had slept for at least fourteen hours. He got to his feet and padded across to the window.

Clouds hung threateningly over the fields, rain dripped from the gutters, and when he looked out into the courtyard, there were brown leaves crawling across the ground and the first bare branches were visible. He started to dress quickly. As he pulled on his boots, the door opened and Joshua entered carrying a jug of hot coffee and a cup on a tray.

'I heard you get out of bed, Colonel,' he said, pouring the coffee. 'How do you feel?

'A lot better than I've got a right to expect,' Clay told him. He sipped some of the coffee. 'That tastes good.'

He put down the cup and started to button his shirt. It was then he noticed the grave expression on Joshua's face. 'What's wrong? Anything happened?'

Joshua sighed heavily. 'I'm so afraid so, Colonel. I went down to the village just before noon to buy some supplies at the store. There was a killing in Cohan's bar.'

Rain tapped against the window with ghostly fingers in the silence, and Clay said, softly, 'Do you know who it was?'

Joshua nodded. 'A man called Varley, one of Sir George Hamilton's men. Apparently he was the one who knifed Shaun Rogan in that fight the other night.'

'Who killed him?' Clay asked tonelessly.

'Kevin Rogan,' Joshua replied. 'He was having a drink in the bar with his brother Dennis. According to Cohan, Varley and some of his friends came in and a fight started. Varley drew a pistol, but Kevin Rogan kicked it out of his hand and brained him with a chair.'

'What happened then?' Clay asked.

'Dennis Rogan escaped through the rear entrance. I saw him gallop away. His brother was unconscious when he was carried out. They strapped him across a horse and rode off to Drumore House. Looked all set for a hanging to me, Colonel.'

'It's a bad business,' Clay said. 'Even if Rogan gets a fair trial, he won't stand a chance against the kind of hand Sir George Hamilton can deal.'

He reached for his coat, as hooves clattered across the cobbles of the courtyard. Joshua went to the window. 'It's Miss Hamilton.'

Clay hurried downstairs, and when he entered the kitchen, she was standing by the fire, steam rising from her damp clothes. She turned toward him, face strained and anxious and, pulling her into his arms, he held her close for a moment. 'Clay, something terrible has happened,' she said.

He nodded. 'I know, Joshua was in the village. He's just told me all about it. What's happened to Kevin Rogan? If your uncle allows any harm to come to him, I'll see him answer for it, if it's the last thing I do on top of earth.'

'But there's no question of anything like that,' she said. 'He intends to take Kevin into Galway himself. He said the trial would be a mere formality. With the kind of evidence he'll be able to present, Kevin will hang.'

'That's probably exactly what *will* happen,' Clay said. 'Has there been any news from Shaun Rogan?'

She nodded. 'That's one of the reasons I came to see you. My uncle forbade me to leave the house, so I had to saddle my horse myself and slip out the back way through the orchards. I met Burke's housekeeper on her way down from his cottage. Apparently, Burke was out all night and decided to spend the day in bed. About an hour ago, Shaun Rogan arrived on horseback with his three younger sons and carried him away at gunpoint. They gave her a message for my uncle. If Kevin isn't returned to them by six o'clock, Burke will hang.'

'Saddle Pegeen for me,' Clay said to Joshua. 'It's the sort of thing I would have expected from Shaun Rogan, but how he managed to seat a horse I'll never know.'

'What do you intend to do?' she said.

He shrugged. 'The first step is obviously to see Shaun Rogan to ask him to stay his hand until I can speak to your uncle. I'd like you to come with me. They seem to hold you in some respect.'

'Your difficulty won't be in handling the Rogans,' she said, 'but in making my uncle see sense.'

He tried to sound reassuring and squeezed her shoulders as they went outside to the horses. 'I'll cross that bridge when I come to it.'

It was raining heavily as they crossed the moor, but he paid little heed to it. He was busy with his own thoughts, searching desperately for some solution to a problem that seemed to have only one answer – two men kicking on the end of a rope. If Shaun Rogan and his family were allowed to take the law into their own hands, they were finished. The cavalry would be called in to root them out of their valley once and for all.

As they passed the clump of trees near the head of the valley, Dennis Rogan rode out to join them on a roan mare, a shotgun crooked in one arm. 'Is your father below?' Clay asked.

'That he is, Colonel,' Dennis told him. 'He was hoping for a word with you. I think Marteen was to ride over, but they'll be busy trying to fix my father's leg at the moment.'

'The damned fool,' Clay said. 'I told him to keep out of the saddle.'

Dennis nodded to Joanna and moved back into the trees, and they descended the path and galloped past the paddock into the yard. As they dismounted, the door opened and Cathal ran out and helped Joanna to the ground. Clay unstrapped his saddlebags and walked up the steps into the house without a word.

Shaun Rogan was sprawled in the chair by the fire, his foot was supported on a stool and his trouser leg had been slit to the waist. His wife leaned over him, trying to stem a steady ooze of blood that trickled down into a basin. Burke was trussed to a chair in one corner, ropes twisted cruelly round his limbs so that he could not move. His eyes gleamed when he saw Clay, but he said nothing.

Clay opened his saddlebags and dropped down onto one knee beside Big Shaun. 'I thought I told you to stay off his leg?'

'There was work to be done,' Rogan boomed. 'Important work.' His face twisted with pain and he reached for the whiskey bottle.

Several of the stitches had burst and Clay took out a needle and thread and started to repair the damage. As he worked, he said, 'I'm sorry to hear about Kevin, but you're not helping him by taking the action you have.'

'Let's talk sense, Colonel,' Shaun Rogan said. 'Once they get my lad to Galway Gaol, he's a dead man. Hamilton's men will tell their version of things and no one else who was in the pub will have the guts to say anything different.' He shook his head and said deliberately, 'I've made my decision. If Kevin isn't back here by six, I'll hang that scut Burke. I'll place the noose around his neck myself. No one else need bear the blame, but me.'

Burke laughed harshly. 'If you think Sir George will count me a fair exchange for your son, Rogan, you must think again. The fact that you intend to hang me will suit him very well. Afterwards, he'll have the pleasure of seeing you all kick air.'

'He's right, Mr Rogan,' Joanna put in desperately. 'I know my uncle and the way his mind works. By hanging Burke, you'll be playing right into his hands.'

As Clay knotted the bandage into place, Shaun Rogan shook his head. 'I'll not stand by and see my son hanging for killing a man in self-defence. Varley drew on him, there was nothing else Kevin could have done.' He emptied the bottle and placed it deliberately down upon the floor. 'I'll not go back on what I've said. If Kevin isn't here by six o'clock, Burke hangs.'

Clay got to his feet and slung his saddlebags over his shoulder. 'You owe me a favour, Big Shaun, and you can repay it easily. I'm going to Hamilton to see what can be done. I want you to promise me you won't make a move before midnight.'

There was a strained silence, and Mrs Rogan crossed quickly to her husband and placed a wrinkled hand timidly on his shoulders. 'Trust the colonel, Shaun. He's proved a true friend.'

Shaun Rogan still hesitated, and Clay said impatiently, 'For God's sake, make up your mind as to what you really want. Your son returned to you in one piece or Burke hanging lifeless at the end of a rope. It's not much of an exchange.'

Big Shaun slammed a hand against the arm of his chair. 'By God, Colonel, it isn't. I'll wait till midnight, but no later.'

Joanna sobbed with relief and Clay turned and smiled briefly at her. 'I'd like you to stay here, just to make sure Big Shaun knows what time it is.'

She nodded, eyes dark in a white face. 'Of course, Clay, if you want me to.'

He moved closer and squeezed her hand. 'Don't worry,' he said softly. 'I'll manage something.' He turned away from the new hope which sparked in her eyes, and went outside to Pegeen.

Once on top of the moor, he gave the mare her head and galloped through the rain, his mind concentrated on the conflict ahead. Already a plan was forming in his head and yet he had to meet Sir George Hamilton first to see if things could be handled sensibly.

He came down from the moor through the gap in the wall and cantered across the grass. As he passed the stables at the rear, he saw that a carriage was being got ready and that at least a dozen men were saddling their horses.

He dismounted at the foot of the steps and went up to the front door. As he raised his hand to the bell-chain, the door was opened by the butler. At the same moment, a hand pulled him out of the way and Sir George Hamilton appeared.

When he spoke, his voice was icy. 'You are no longer welcome in my house, Colonel Fitzgerald.'

'And I have no wish to be here,' Clay said. 'But there's something much more important to discuss. Are you aware that the Rogans hold your man Burke and intend to hang him if Kevin Rogan is not with them by six o'clock?'

'I have already been informed of the situation,' Sir George said. 'Naturally, I'm extremely sorry about Burke, but under the circumstances, there is nothing to be done. It's much more important to the peace of the county that a notorious malcontent like Kevin Rogan should be safely lodged in gaol. I intend to escort him to Galway myself within the hour. Afterwards, I hope to return with sufficient help to root his damned family out of Hidden Valley once and for all.'

Clay almost lost control. 'You wanted something like this to happen, didn't you? If they hang Burke, you'll be able to see the rest of them laid by the heels.'

'Exactly!' Sir George said, and something unholy glowed deep in his eyes. 'I'll see them under the sod, every one of them, if it's the last thing I do.'

For a moment, Clay gazed into insane eyes, and then he turned and went down the steps to Pegeen. As he swung into the saddle, he heard Sir George say to the butler, 'If that man ever puts foot on my land again, set the dogs on him. Do you understand?' The door closed and Clay cantered away across the grass.

He had expected little from the interview and had discovered nothing new except that Sir George was unbalanced, which was something he had suspected from the first. Probably the knowledge of his disease and eventual death had preyed on the man's mind. Out of his despair had grown the need to vent his rage and fear on someone else. The Rogans fitted the bill to perfection.

There remained only one course of action, and Clay smiled sardonically as he rode into the stables at Claremont. What was it Morgan used to say? 'In war, always make your first move something so audacious, the enemy would never expect it in a thousand years. After that, play the cards as they fall.'

Morgan had lived by his maxim with some success, but he had also died by it, Clay reflected grimly, as he went into the kitchen and dropped his saddlebags on the table. Joshua turned from the stove, sleeves rolled up. 'Just in time for a meal, Colonel.'

'I've got to go straight out again,' Clay told him, 'but I could eat something quick and drink a cup of coffee.'

He went up to his room and took off his coat. Then he opened the trunk and pulled out the grey cavalry greatcoat. As he buttoned it to his neck, thunder echoed menacingly in the distance and the sky darkened. The rain increased with a sudden rush, and he nodded in satisfaction. It suited his plans perfectly. He belted the black holster around his waist and remembered that the Colt was in his bag downstairs. As he placed the felt campaign hat on his head and faced the mirror, the figure that stared out at him assumed an identity of its own and he shivered slightly and turned and left the room.

Joshua had the coffee and food waiting for him on the table and Clay took the Colt from his bag and checked its action. As he gulped down the coffee, he explained the situation and Joshua's face turned grave. 'I don't like it, Colonel. I don't like it one little bit. They'll be expecting trouble.'

'I don't think so,' Clay said. 'The Rogans are holding Burke. What else can they do?'

'It's beginning to get too dangerous, Colonel,' Joshua said. 'This time someone will get suspicious about you for sure.'

'I've thought about that,' Clay admitted. 'And there's a certain element of risk, but I must take the chance.' He finished his coffee and slapped Joshua on the shoulder. 'Don't worry, I'll be back. To tell you the truth, I'm almost beginning to enjoy myself. Old habits die hard.'

Joshua nodded soberly. 'That's exactly what's bothering me, Colonel. You think twice about each move you make and then think again.' He was standing in the doorway, face grave and troubled, as Clay rode out of the stables through the heavy rain and moved up through the trees to the moor.

The solution was to be found somewhere along the route to Galway, that much was obvious, and the nearer to Drumore, the better. He galloped through the heavy rain, following the track he had taken on the night he had ridden to Kileen to deal with Marley, but as he turned down through the trees to join the Galway Road, he was still no nearer an answer.

It was shortly after six o'clock as he skirted Kileen, moving through the woods that filled the valley, one hand up to ward off the wet branches that whipped against his face. When he was well beyond the village, he turned back onto the road, and a few moments later, came to a stone bridge that spanned a brawling torrent of water.

At some time, the centre of the bridge had been swept away by heavy flooding and a temporary repair had been made with stout planks. Already the swollen, foam-flecked stream was lapping through the cracks, and as Clay dismounted and went forward to examine them, a plan began to form in his mind.

Kileen was perhaps a quarter of a mile away and he turned into the trees and rode back toward the village. He recalled that a public house, a replica of Cohan's, stood at the far end of the single street and he approached it cautiously from the rear and tethered Pegeen to a bush beside a high wall which enclosed the yard.

There was a gap in the wall and, pulling the black scarf up over his face, he squeezed through and crossed to the back door. It opened to his touch and he stepped into a stone-flagged kitchen and drew his Colt.

The room was empty, but a stout wooden door stood ajar on the far side and he could hear a murmur of voices. He listened to them for a moment and then opened the door wide and stepped through into the bar.

The publican was in the act of turning, a jug in one hand. He stood quite still and an expression of ludicrous dismay appeared on his face. 'Captain Swing!' he whispered.

Two men sat in the inglenook by the fire. One was old, with long white hair and a face like a russet apple. Clay saw, with a sense of shock, that the other was Father Costello.

As they turned to look at him, he said softly in

an Irish accent, 'No trouble now and you won't come to any harm.'

The publican backed away to join the other two by the fire, and Father Costello said quietly, 'These are good people, my friend. I can vouch for that.'

The publican seemed to have recovered from his first shock and now his face was alive and interested. 'Glory be, Captain, Father Costello speaks nothing but the truth. We're all Irishmen here and to hell with the bloody British Empire!'

'Up the Republic!' the old man cackled, and Father Costello laid a hand gently on his arm.

'I intend harm to no man here,' Clay said. 'But I need your help. In fact I'll have to insist on it.' He looked directly at the publican. 'How many customers do you expect within the next half-hour?'

The man shrugged. 'The local lads usually come in at eight. There might be the odd one before then, but I wouldn't bank on it in weather like this.'

Clay nodded in satisfaction. 'That suits me perfectly. Have you got a horse in the stables at the back?'

The publican nodded and there was pride in his voice. 'You could call her that. As fine a mare as you'll see in a day's ride. She won me twenty pounds at Galway Fair this summer.'

'Would you lend her to save a man's life?' Clay asked.

The publican frowned and then his nostrils flared. 'By God, I will, if you say the word, Captain. We owe you that and more in Kileen after the way you handled Squire Marley for us.'

'Good man!' Clay said. 'Now this is what I want you to do. Sometime during the next hour at the outside, Sir George Hamilton will pass through Kileen in his coach with an armed guard. They carry Kevin Rogan to Galway to see him hanged.'

Father Costello's breath hissed sharply between his teeth and the old man crossed himself and muttered, 'God save us all!'

'When they arrive,' Clay went on, 'I want you to go out and stop the coach. Tell Sir George the bridge is down and that men are trying to repair it. He wants to reach Galway tonight, so I'm hoping he'll send most of his men to help with the work on the bridge while he waits here with Rogan.'

'If Kevin Rogan has killed a man, he must stand trial,' Father Costello said quietly.

Clay shook his head. 'If he isn't home by midnight, his father intends to hang Peter Burke, Father. Take your choice.'

Pain appeared on the priest's face, and the publican said hesitantly, 'It's not that I'm afraid for myself, you understand, Captain, but I've a daughter away in Galway town to think of. What will Sir George do to me when he finds I've helped trick him?'

Before Clay could answer, Father Costello said quietly, 'It has occurred to me that if we fail to fall in with your plans, you may offer us some violence, Captain. Is this not so?'

Clay saw his drift immediately. 'Naturally, Father.'

The priest sighed. 'Then it would seem I have no option but to go out and speak with Sir George if only to save my two companions here from your wrath.'

The publican smiled and turned to Clay. 'I'll saddle the mare for you, Captain.' Clay told him where to leave her, and the man went out, closing the door behind him.

As Clay peered out of the window into the darkening street, the priest said, 'This is a bad business.'

Clay nodded. 'I can see no answer to the situation except that Ireland be given her freedom. Violence begets violence, Father.'

'But does a sensible man need to have any part

of it?' Father Costello asked mildly. 'Surely there are other ways of spending one's life?'

'It depends on your point of view,' Clay said. 'Not so long ago, I met a man who contended that as life is action and passion, it is required of a man that he should share the passion and action of his times at peril of being judged not to have lived.'

Father Costello nodded. 'An interesting observation. The trouble is that human beings hate each other so easily. How often, I wonder, has the rebel burned down a man's house, not for political reasons, but for private vengeance?'

'And there you've come to the kernel of the problem,' Clay said. To his horror, he realized he had spoken in his normal voice.

The priest did not seem to have noticed. 'One thing, sir. I want you to give me your word you will do no killing here this night.'

Clay turned and his smile was hidden by the scarf. 'I may have to crack a head or two, Father,' he said. 'But no more than that.'

The publican came back into the room. 'That's all set then, Captain.'

'One more thing,' Clay said. 'Have you a sharp knife handy? I fancy his hands will be bound.'

The publican produced one from beneath the bar

and Clay said, 'You stand there. When they come through the bar, I'll push Rogan toward you. You can sever his bonds while I deal with the others.'

At that moment, there was the unmistakable sound of wheels coming along the village street and he turned to the window. The coach approached slowly through the mud, armed horsemen at front and rear.

Father Costello got to his feet and smiled gently. 'It would seem that the time has come for my performance.' He paused with the door half-open and looked directly at Clay. 'Remember your promise,' he said, and then the door closed behind him.

The cavalcade stopped as he held up his hand, and it was impossible to hear what was said. Father Costello went to the door of the coach and Sir George appeared, a frown on his face. After a while, he gave an order. Four of his men dismounted, the others rode off toward the bridge. The door opened and Father Costello moved back inside and walked across to the fire, hands outstretched to the blaze. Clay waited behind the door, and Kevin Rogan was pushed inside and Sir George followed him, a pistol in one hand.

Rogan's hands were twisted behind him and bound securely with rope. Clay put a foot in his back, sending him hurtling across the bar, pushed Sir George sideways with one powerful swing and rammed the door in the face of the man who followed.

He shot the bolt and turned, as Sir George raised himself on one elbow and fired. The bullet hit Clay in the upper part of his left arm and the shock of it stopped him dead in his tracks. As pain flooded through him, he kicked the pistol from Sir George's hand and ran for the door at the back of the bar.

Kevin was already into the kitchen, hands free, and Clay followed, pushing him across the yard and through the gap in the wall. It was almost dark and the horses whinnied a greeting from the gloom. Clay swung into the saddle and, a moment later, moved away through the woods, Kevin at his heels.

They splashed across the ford on the outskirts of the village and took the track which led up onto the moor. Behind them, faintly through the rain, they could hear an outcry from Kileen, and Clay grinned through the pain. In any event, Morgan's maxim had proved true and a bullet was a small price to pay.

He reined in Pegeen and Kevin Rogan moved beside him. 'Why are we stopping here?' he demanded from the darkness.

'Because this is where we part company,' Clay told him. 'I've saved your life, Rogan. Now it's your turn to do something for me. Your father holds Peter Burke hostage for your safe return. If you're not home by midnight, Burke hangs.'

'But you're wounded,' Kevin said. 'At least let me bind it for you.'

'Get home, man!' Clay cried in a voice of iron. He slapped Rogan's mare across the rump, sending her forward into the night, and turned Pegeen away across the moor.

After a while, he stopped and, removing the black scarf, knotted it about his wound and then rode on, alone with the heavy rain and the night.

It was a nightmare ride and he urged Pegeen forward, his knees desperately gripping her sides. He must have been riding for an hour when she tripped over a tussock and threw him from the saddle.

He was never very clear afterwards as to how long he had lain there. He remembered the mare standing over him, her tongue rough on his face, and then he was up and heaving himself back into the saddle.

It was Pegeen who brought him home a good hour later. She crossed the cobbled yard, hooves soundless in the rush of the rain, and halted in the stables. For a little while, Clay sat there and then he slid from the saddle and lurched across the yard to the door, sick and faint with pain.

The kitchen was in darkness and he wondered vaguely whether Joshua was asleep. As the storm raged outside, the very air seemed electric and humming with energy, as if there was nothing sleeping, as if in the surrounding darkness, there was a presence that waited for something to happen. And then the lightning flared outside and in the split second of its illumination, he saw Joshua, Kevin Rogan and Joanna facing him across the table.

What happened after that was confused and disjointed. Joanna was beside him, her face surprisingly calm, and Kevin stripped the wet clothes from Clay's body while Joshua heated water. They wrapped Clay in a blanket by the fire and Joanna held a brandy bottle to his lips and told him to swallow.

He coughed as the fierce warmth of the raw spirit surged through him and then Joshua placed a bowl of water on the table and opened Clay's instrument case. 'We've got to get that bullet out, Colonel.'

Clay took a deep breath and fought to control himself. 'I don't think the arm is broken. It was a small-bore pistol. You'll have to probe, though. Just above the elbow. You've done it before.'

Kevin held his arm and Clay took some more brandy and watched with a detached, professional interest as Joshua started.

Joshua gently cleansed the area of the wound and felt for the bullet with no success. He then reached for a probe and inserted it carefully into the opening, pushing it in various directions until the porcelain tip grated on the bullet. After a while, he looked up at Clay. 'Sorry, Colonel. I'm going to have to cut.'

Clay nodded weakly. 'You're the doctor. Remember your lessons.'

He drank some more brandy as Joshua reached for a scalpel. Joshua paused for a moment, sweat glistening on his brow in the firelight, and then he cut down through the flesh onto the end of the probe.

The pain which coursed through Clay was so exquisite that he gave an involuntary gasp of agony, and Joanna tightened her hand on his shoulder. As he opened his eyes again, Joshua lifted out the bullet with his fingers and dropped it into the fireplace. He washed his hands in the basin and forced a smile, 'Got to stitch it now, Colonel.'

'Stitch away, by all means,' Clay told him and braced himself, but nature pushes no man too far, and at the first touch of the needle, he lapsed into a merciful darkness.

10

Clay awakened to firelight writhing and twisting in fantastic shapes across his bedroom ceiling. For a moment, he lay there, his mind a blank, and then he remembered and pain flooded through him as he tried to move his left arm.

He groaned, and immediately a cool hand was laid across his brow. He turned his head and found Joanna sitting by the bed, her face half-hidden by the shadows.

'How do you feel?' she said.

'Not too good at the moment. What time is it?'

She told him it was almost two o'clock and he lay there in silence, trying to focus his mind upon the events of the previous hours. After a while he said, 'They released Burke, I hope?'

She nodded. 'The moment Kevin arrived.'

There was another small space of silence before he said, 'How did you find out about me?'

She shrugged. 'You couldn't really expect to keep it a secret this time – certainly not from the Rogans or me. The connection was so obvious. But it was Kevin who clinched it. He recognized Pegeen.'

Clay sighed. 'It was bound to come out sooner or later.'

'What made you do it?' she said gently.

He shook his head. 'I don't really know. At first I tried to tell myself it was because of Marley – that he needed to be taught a lesson. But now I'm not sure. Kevin Rogan told me the other night that no man could live in this country and stay neutral; that sooner or later I would have to take sides or get out, and he was right. The things I've seen here, the squalor, the poverty, the degradation – these things are caused by men like your uncle and Marley. I despise them and everything they stand for.'

She squeezed his hand and tears glistened in her eyes. 'I know, Clay, I know. But what can you do? What can anyone do about it? Men like my uncle and Marley have the weight of the law and the power of the British nation behind them. You're a soldier. Do you honestly think that Ireland has the slightest hope of winning her freedom by force of arms?'

He shook his head. 'Of course not, but there are other ways. If a loud enough cry is raised, the English themselves may do something about the situation. I hardly think your uncle and Marley are representative.'

'And yet men like Kevin Rogan will continue to fight,' she said. 'The Fenians will rebel, if not this year, then next year. The innocent will die as well as the guilty, outrage will follow outrage until what little sympathy Ireland can command will be dissipated.'

He knew in his heart that what she said was true and, touched by the desolation in her voice, he took one of her hands and said gently, 'There is always hope – that's the only thing these people have to live for. That, and a pride in their race.'

She pushed back a tendril of dark hair from her forehead and stood up. 'I'll have to be going. Even if my uncle has returned home instead of continuing to Galway, I may be lucky enough to get to my room unobserved. I'm in the west wing, some distance away from his rooms, and I have a key to a small door that leads into the stable yard.'

'What about Kevin?' he said. 'Has he left?'

She nodded. 'He knows of a place a mile or two from the farm where he'll be safe for a day or two.'

'They'll have to get him out of the country as quickly as possible. Your uncle is bound to call in the constabulary over this matter.'

'And what about you?' she said gravely. 'Hasn't it occurred to you that Burke will suspect who you are, especially when he hears from my uncle the full details of what happened in Kileen, and starts putting two and two together.'

Clay tried to sit up against the pillows. 'Suspicion is one thing, proof is another matter. After all, I do have a certain standing. A gentleman doesn't ride the countryside by night wearing a black mask and using such a ridiculously melodramatic name as Captain Swing.'

She pulled on her gloves and there was no smile on her face. 'I hope you know what you're doing, Clay. For some reason, I'm frightened – really frightened. Recently, my uncle seems to have got worse. At times I don't think he's in his right mind.'

Clay managed a confident smile. 'There's nothing for you to worry about, I promise you.'

There was a quiet tap on the door and it opened to admit Joshua. His teeth gleamed in the firelight. 'I heard you talking, Colonel. Can I get you anything?'

'You can saddle Pegeen and escort Miss Hamilton home,' Clay told him. Joanna started to protest and he raised a hand to silence her. 'No, I insist. You can take the path across the moor. I'll not rest easy until I know you're safely home.'

Joshua withdrew and Joanna sat on the edge of the bed and smiled. 'All right, I surrender.'

Clay smiled back at her and she leaned forward and kissed him full on the mouth. He slipped his good arm about her shoulders, but she pulled away and moved across to the door.

'When will I see you again?' Clay said.

'It may be difficult for me to get away for the next day or two,' she said. 'If anything happens that I think you should know about, I'll send a message. There's a young stable boy called Joseph. I can trust him.' She smiled once and then the door closed softly behind her.

He listened to the sound of the horses moving across the yard through the heavy rain and thought about what she had said. That Burke would suspect was a foregone conclusion, but that he would dare to bring his suspicions into the open was another matter entirely.

Clay chuckled, and realized with something of a surprise that he did not fear the prospect of crossing swords again with either Burke or his master. Riding roughshod over half-starved peasants was one thing, but making public accusations against an American citizen with the kind of connections and bank balance Clay had, was quite another.

He suddenly realized just how much he had come to dislike Sir George Hamilton and his agent, and as he drifted into sleep, he sighed ruefully. Kevin Rogan had been right in his prophecy. No man could sit on the fence forever.

It was shortly after nine when he awakened to pale autumn sunlight filtering in through the window. Joshua was in the act of putting a log on the fire, and the blankets draped across a chair by the bed showed where he had spent the night. He turned and came forward with a smile, 'How do you feel, Colonel?'

Clay struggled to sit up. There was a steady, dull ache in his left arm and he felt a little light-headed, but otherwise fine. 'I could do with something to eat.'

'I'll see to that right away, Colonel.'

Clay nodded. 'First, you can fix me a tub of hot water in front of the fire downstairs. I'm getting up.'

Joshua's smile disappeared. 'But that's crazy, Colonel. You need a few days in bed.'

'I rode for three days with a minie ball in my left foot after Chancellorsville,' Clay said. 'As I remember, there wasn't a bed to be had for miles.' He shrugged. 'In any case I must look as normal as possible in case we have any unexpected visitors. Can't have them finding me in bed with a gunshot wound.'

Joshua sighed and his face was troubled. 'You got a point there, Colonel.' He shook his head despondently as he opened the door. 'I knew things would get complicated. I knew it in my bones from the beginning.'

Clay lay there for another hour, before Joshua came back into the room and helped him out of bed and down to the kitchen, where the tub was steaming before a roaring fire.

He soaked in it for half an hour, his wounded arm propped on one side out of the water and drank two cups of coffee laced with brandy. Then he dried off and Joshua helped him to dress in fresh linen. He gently eased his wounded arm through the sleeve of a tweed riding jacket and sat down at the table to eat.

As he was finishing his meal, there was a clatter of hooves on the cobbles outside and Joshua moved quickly to the window. He turned, relief on his face. 'It's a boy on a pony, Colonel. I've never seen him before.'

Clay frowned. 'I think he'll prove to be a messenger from Miss Hamilton. Let him in.'

Joshua opened the door and the boy moved hesitantly inside. He was perhaps thirteen, tall and lanky for his age, his freckled, alert face topped by a shock of sandy hair. 'You'll be Joseph,' Clay said. 'Have you a message for me?'

The boy nodded. 'If you are Colonel Fitzgerald, sir.' From the inside pocket of his shabby tweed coat, he produced an envelope sealed with red wax. 'Miss Hamilton asked me to bring this to you and tell no one.'

Clay slit open the letter with a table knife, and as he read, his face turned grave. When he had finished, he slipped the letter into his pocket and got to his feet. 'Saddle Pegeen for me,' he said to

Joshua. 'I'm going out.' For a moment, Joshua looked as if he intended to argue, but he appeared to think better of it and left the room.

Clay produced half a sovereign, which he held between finger and thumb. 'Do you know what this is?' The boy's eyes went round and he nodded. 'Come back in three hours and carry a message to Miss Hamilton for me and I'll give you another to match it.'

He flipped the coin into the air and the boy caught it neatly in his hat. 'I'll be here, sir, you can depend on that,' he said with a grin and disappeared through the doorway.

Clay went up to his bedroom for his hat and the Dragoon, and when he came back downstairs, Pegeen was saddled and waiting for him. As Clay mounted, Joshua said, 'Sure I can't come with you, Colonel? You don't look too good to me.'

Clay shook his head. 'With any luck I'll be back in a couple of hours. I'm going to see Shaun Rogan. I'll tell you about it when I return.'

Leaves from the beech trees carpeted the path before him as he cantered up out of the valley. He rode with his left hand thrust deep into his jacket pocket, to support the arm which should really have been in a sling, and schooled his thoughts to ignore the steady, persistent throbbing of his wound.

It was one of those quiet autumn mornings, with the scent of wood smoke in the air and a peculiar heavy stillness over everything. He gave Pegeen her head and thundered along the track, not even pausing when Marteen Rogan rode out of the beech trees at the head of the valley and waved to him.

When he entered the farmyard, Cathal and Dennis were waiting in front of the door to greet him and Clay dismounted and walked forward, feeling more than a little light-headed.

'Is Kevin here?' he said.

Cathal shook his head. 'He's taking it easy a mile or two away in a place we know of, waiting to see which way the wind blows.'

'I never expected to see you on your feet this day, after what Kevin told us,' Dennis said. 'And that's a fact.'

Clay managed a tight smile. 'I'm not too sure how long I can keep it up, but I had to see your father.'

Cathal led the way inside without another word and Clay followed. Shaun Rogan was sprawled comfortably in a chair by the fire, leg raised. As they entered, he turned with a frown and then something sparked in his eyes. 'By God, Colonel, of all the men on earth this day, you are the one I wanted to see most. But shouldn't you be in bed, man?'

Clay pulled forward a chair and sat down opposite him, face grave. 'Something important came up. I had to see you.'

Shaun Rogan reached for the whiskey bottle. He filled a glass and pushed it across. 'Here, drink that to start with. You look as if you could do with it.'

Clay drained the glass in one easy swallow and said quietly, 'Have you had any dealings with a man called Fitzgibbon?'

Rogan frowned and nodded slowly. 'An old friend of mine, a banker in Galway town.' He hesitated for a moment and then went on. 'He holds the mortgage on this property.'

Clay shook his head slowly. 'Not any more. He died two days ago. His nephew has already agreed to dispose of the mortgage to Sir George Hamilton.'

There was a terrible silence in the room and a great vein in the old man's temple throbbed steadily. His tongue flickered across dry lips as he said, 'It can't be true. I know Hamilton had tried to buy the mortgage on several occasions, but Fitzgibbon always refused. He was too good a friend to me.'

'Apparently, his nephew isn't as sentimental,' Clay said drily. 'He's the sole heir and intends to settle the estate as quickly as possible. He sent a special messenger from Galway yesterday afternoon, who found Sir George at the pub in Kileen and delivered the letter asking him if he was still interested in the property. Sir George wrote his acceptance at once and returned the man to Galway, post-haste.'

The old man seemed momentarily dazed. 'But it can't be true,' he said. 'It isn't possible.'

'I'm afraid it is,' Clay said gently. 'Miss Hamilton overheard her uncle and Burke discussing the matter this morning. She sent one of the stable boys over with a letter giving me full details.'

Cathal leaned forward, hands on the table and said quietly, 'Let's not be too hasty, Father. A mortgage is a legal document with clauses in it giving you time to pay and so on. Hamilton can't just walk in and take over without so much as a by-your-leave.'

Shaun Rogan looked up, and all at once he

seemed an old man. 'I'm already two months overdue on my last payment. Fitzgibbon didn't press me.' He made a futile gesture with his hands. 'We needed money for the cause. I've paid for some of the arms which have been landed out of my own pocket, hoping to be reimbursed when the contributions to the fighting fund started to come in.'

Dennis slammed a clenched fist against the table. 'What are we going to do, then?' he demanded. 'Sit here like sheep and let Hamilton and his butchers ride in and take over?'

Shaun Rogan shook his head. 'We'll think of something, lad. We'll think of something.' He turned to Cathal. 'Get on your horse and go for Kevin. We need all the help we can get.'

'I'll be returning to Claremont,' Clay said. 'Joanna has no information as to when they intend to move against you, but she promised to keep me informed. I'll be seeing her messenger again in a couple of hours.'

Rogan's eyes narrowed. 'He may have some news for us.' He turned to Dennis. 'You ride with the colonel to Claremont. After he's spoken with this messenger, you can come back with any news there is.'

Dennis turned without a word and went outside to saddle his horse and Clay got to his feet. 'I have a feeling things are warming up,' he said. 'The next few hours will see great changes in Drumore, though in what way, I'm not quite sure. I'd offer the mortgage myself. I could well afford it, but I smell a plot here between young Fitzgibbon and Hamilton.'

Shaun Rogan seemed to have recovered himself and nodded soberly. 'We're all in God's hands, Colonel, but one thing is certain. I've lived here all my life. Whatever happens, I intend to die here.' For a moment, Clay gazed into those calm eyes, and then he turned and left the room.

He and Dennis rode quickly up to the head of the valley and galloped across the moors, pausing only to explain what was happening to Marteen.

Down below them through the trees, a band of white mist floated above a stream, and all at once there seemed a chill in the air. Clay rode in silence, occupied with his own thoughts, wondering if Joanna had managed to find out anything more about her uncle's plans. He thought of her alone in that great house, with no one to whom she could turn, and a feeling of inexpressible tenderness swept through him. He slowed Pegeen to a walk as they passed along a narrow path through trees and entered a clearing.

Peter Burke sat his horse and waited for them. He was dressed very correctly in a fine broadcloth riding coat, and his boots were highly polished. He raised his crop to the brim of his hat and said gravely, 'Good morning to you, Colonel Fitzgerald.'

Clay's hand slid into his coat pocket for the Dragoon Colt, but half a dozen men rode out of the trees into the clearing, shotguns ready.

One side of Burke's face was still bruised and swollen from the fight, and his eyes glittered malevolently as he urged his horse forward and held out a hand. 'I'll take your pistol, Colonel, if you please.'

Clay handed it across, and behind him, Dennis cursed as one of the men snatched his shotgun away from him. There was a moment's silence and Clay gazed around him at the circle of unfriendly faces and said calmly, 'Now what?'

Burke moved closer and started to search his pockets without a word. Within a moment, he had found Joanna's letter. Clay sat there, anger rising inside him as Burke's dark eyes flickered across the page. When he had finished, he carefully folded the letter and placed it in his inside pocket without any comment. 'We'll go to Drumore House now, Colonel. Sir George desires a word with you. I'd strongly advise you against trying to escape. It would give me great pleasure to see you both blasted from the saddle. I'd like you to believe that.'

Dennis began an angry retort and Clay leaned forward quickly and laid a hand on the boy's arm. 'Do as he asks. Our turn will come later.' There was ugly laughter from some of the men and, ignoring it, he urged Pegeen forward along the track, taking the lead.

They crossed the moor at the back of Claremont and skirted the village, coming down to Drumore House through the orchards. Clay and Dennis dismounted and were hustled through a door and along a stone-flagged passage, finally stopping outside the conservatory door.

Burke went in and they waited. After a while, he came out again and led the way through the hall into the long room with the French windows, in which the reception had been held.

One of the men closed the door and another pushed Dennis into the centre of the room. Burke said carelessly over his shoulder, 'Watch the colonel,' and as he advanced on the boy, the men closed in around Clay.

Dennis had turned bone-white and suddenly looked very young. As he watched him, Clay thought of that first day on the Galway Road and of the dash and bravado that had faded so quickly when the youth had been faced with the harsh reality of violence.

Burke said calmly, 'I want to know where that brother of yours is hiding.'

Dennis licked his lips and Clay said quietly and clearly, his words cutting through the stillness, 'Remember your name and nation, lad.'

Dennis drew himself erect, nostrils flaring, a new expression appearing on his face. 'Yes, by God, I'm a Rogan, but I'm an Irishman first and I'll not betray my own kind like you have, ye scut.'

Burke hit him in the stomach, and as the lad keeled over, a fist of iron smashed into his mouth, lifting him backwards.

Dennis groaned and tried to get up. Slowly and painfully, he pushed himself onto one knee, his mouth ragged and bloody. Burke hauled him easily to his feet with one hand. 'Has your memory improved?' he asked calmly.

Dennis seemed to be trying to speak. His mouth

worked and a ghastly grin appeared and then he spat into Burke's face. The land agent felled the boy with one blow and lifted back a boot to strike. Clay ducked under an arm and, flinging himself forward, caught Burke by the shoulder and sent him staggering across the room. There was a growl of rage from the men behind, but as they moved forward threateningly, the door opened and Sir George entered.

He surveyed the scene calmly and, ignoring Clay, crossed the floor and examined Dennis. 'Did he tell you?' he asked Burke.

The agent wiped blood and spittle from his face with a handkerchief and shook his head. 'I'd only just started, but he's stubborn.'

Sir George nodded. 'There are surer ways. Have two of the men take him upstairs. Clean him up and make sure he's sensible when I need him.'

Burke gave the necessary order and Dennis was escorted from the room. As the door closed, Sir George turned and regarded Clay coldly for several moments, and then he walked slowly forward and struck him in the face. 'You made a fool of me, Colonel, but it's my turn to laugh now.'

He snapped his fingers and one of the men opened the door and went out. A moment later, he returned with a bundle, which he handed to Burke. Burke opened it slowly and dropped onto the floor at Clay's feet, one by one, his old felt campaign hat, the black scarf, and the Confederate cavalry greatcoat.

Burke said, 'The fact that Kevin Rogan was rescued after your visit to the Rogan farm yesterday set me thinking, Colonel. I should have guessed it before. Several people described how the moonlight glinted on the brass frame of Captain Swing's Colt, but a Navy Colt doesn't have a brass frame.'

'How very interesting,' Clay said.

'Oh, it was,' Burke told him. 'You see I remembered reading somewhere how the Confederates were short of metal during the war. They melted down the brass church bells at a place called Macon in Georgia and manufactured a copy of the Navy Colt, using the brass for the frame of the weapon. They called it a Dragoon Colt, I understand, and it was issued extensively to Confederate cavalry units.' His hand came out of his pocket and he was holding Clay's pistol.

'Even when Burke told me of this, I still found it difficult to believe,' Sir George said. 'That's why we played our little game this morning.' He took

Joanna's letter from his pocket and held it up, hand shaking. 'I've been kept well-informed of my niece's attachment for you, believe me, sir. This morning I was testing her as well as you when I allowed her to overhear Burke and myself discussing the new turn that events have taken with the death of James Fitzgibbon.'

'Miss Hamilton was carefully watched,' Burke said. 'We wanted her to get in touch with you. When she did, she unknowingly played right into our hands. You rode straight to the Rogans to warn them, as I had expected, leaving only your servant at home, which was something else I had hoped for.' He stirred the clothing on the floor with one foot. 'The final proof, Colonel Fitzgerald.'

'The proof that will hang you, by God, you damned rebel,' Sir George said, and there was a slight trace of foam on his lips.

Clay shrugged and said lightly, 'There must be other ex-Confederate officers in Ireland, more than one Dragoon Colt. I hope you know what you're doing.'

Burke moved close to him, a pale smile on his face. 'We do indeed, Colonel. How is your arm this morning, by the way? Not too painful, I trust?' He gripped Clay's left arm slightly above the elbow and squeezed for a moment, and Clay's eyes closed as the agony flooded through him.

Sir George laughed coldly. 'I think perhaps the colonel would like a seat.' Someone pulled one forward and Clay was thrust down into it. The baronet continued. 'Half an hour ago, I sent a special messenger mounted on my best horse to the constabulary headquarters in Galway. I've told them that I've captured Captain Swing. I've pointed out that the situation in this district is bad and have asked them to send an escort of cavalry to take you into Galway. I have also said that I expect to have Kevin Rogan in my hands by the time they arrive here.'

Clay looked up and said grimly, 'You'll never take Kevin Rogan alive again.'

'Ah, but I'm afraid you underestimate the strength of brotherly love,' Sir George said. 'I've sent the stable lad, Joseph – you've met him already, I understand – with a message to Shaun Rogan. I've told him that Dennis Rogan is in my hands, that I'll exchange him for his brother Kevin. If he refuses, I'll hand Dennis over to the cavalry as a confederate of Captain Swing. No judge in the land will believe the lad wasn't, by the time Burke and I have given our evidence.'

He laughed, and the foam on his lips was more apparent. Some of the men shuffled nervously and Sir George said, 'Take him away. Lock him up securely with the other until I send for him again.'

Burke pulled Clay up from the chair and pushed him roughly toward the door. One of the men opened it and they passed out into the hall. As Burke led the way up the great staircase, Clay said, 'What happened to my servant?'

Burke shrugged carelessly. 'A crack on the head. No more than that. I've heard tell black men have hard skulls.'

They passed along a wide corridor in silence, mounted a narrower flight of stairs and then another until they were on the third storey.

The two men who had originally left with Dennis lounged outside a stout door bound with iron bands, and Burke said, 'Is he all right?'

One of them nodded. 'Still in the land of the living, more's the pity, Mr Burke.'

The key was in the lock and Burke turned it and opened the door. 'In you go, Colonel, and I wouldn't waste your time in trying to find a way to escape. It doesn't exist.'

Clay moved forward and paused, looking directly

into the man's face. 'He's insane,' he said. 'You know that, don't you?'

Burke shrugged. 'I don't get paid to think about things like that.'

'Then tell me one thing,' Clay said. 'What's happened to Miss Hamilton?'

Burke laughed harshly. 'Don't you worry about her, Colonel. Whatever she's done, she's still a Hamilton. Sir George will think of something suitable, I suppose. For the moment, she's confined to her rooms. A slight indisposition. Nothing to worry about.'

He pushed Clay forward into the room, and as the door closed, his laughter echoed through the heavy oak planks and then it faded into the distance as he moved away along the corridor.

11

Clay leaned against the window, a cheroot between his teeth, and gazed out through the iron bars to the park, sixty feet below. For more than an hour he had watched the road, waiting for something to happen, but nothing stirred.

Smoke rose into the air from the cottages of Drumore hidden by the trees, and somewhere in the distance a dog barked as it chased a rabbit through the undergrowth. He turned as Dennis groaned. The boy sat on the edge of the narrow bed, head in hands, shoulders hunched dejectedly. 'God save us, Colonel, but me head's going to burst into a thousand pieces at any moment.'

Clay patted him on the shoulder sympathetically.

'He packs a hard punch, lad, there's no denying that.'

Dennis tried to smile and touched his smashed and swollen mouth gingerly with the tips of his fingers. 'What's going to happen to us, Colonel? Will we hang?'

'Having had no previous experience of English justice, I can't say, but I understand rebels against the Crown *have* been known to come to that end.' Clay smiled down at him. 'No sense in worrying about it yet. There's always hope. Perhaps Kevin will come to put himself in your place?'

'To burn the house down is more likely,' Dennis snorted. 'And there's plenty would follow him. He's had enough troubles as it is, trying to hold some of them back until the day fixed for the general rising next year.'

'So you don't think he'll come?' Clay said.

'I'll see him in hell before I let him take my place.' There was a new firmness in the boy's voice, indicating that at least he had passed over into manhood. 'He wouldn't stand a chance, not with this Varley affair hanging over him.'

Clay nodded sombrely. 'You know it and Kevin knows it. The point now is what will he do?'

He turned back to the window and stiffened.

A pony and trap had moved in through the gates below and halted outside the lodge. Shaun Rogan handled the reins, and the stable boy, Joseph, sat beside him.

The old man shaded his eyes with one hand as he gazed up toward the house through the pale autumn sunlight, and then he said something to Joseph. The boy jumped down to the ground and came along the drive at a jog-trot.

Clay said quietly, 'Your father is down at the main gate.'

Dennis got to his feet and stood there, swaying slightly. 'Is he alone?'

Clay shook his head. 'He came with the stable boy who brought him Sir George's message. He's just sent the lad up to the house while he waits. He'll be trying to arrange some sort of truce, I fancy.'

Dennis moved beside him and they both craned their necks and tried to see what was going on down at the front entrance. After a while, Joseph appeared and ran back. They could see him talking quickly and nodding his head and then Shaun Rogan picked up the reins and started toward the house. He halted about forty yards away and waited.

Clay and Dennis turned as the key grated in the lock behind them. The door opened and Burke moved inside. He was holding a pistol in one hand. 'Outside, both of you,' he said. 'Shaun Rogan seems to think we might be pulling some kind of a trick on him. He wants to see you in the flesh.'

He led the way along the corridor, Clay and Dennis following, two armed men behind them. Dennis still seemed unsure on his feet, and Clay placed one arm about the lad's shoulders and steadied him as they descended the great staircase into the entrance hall.

The front door was open and half a dozen men armed with shotguns stood outside. Sir George was waiting a few yards away from the bottom of the steps, looking toward Rogan.

Burke halted Clay and Dennis at the top of the steps and went down to speak to Sir George. Except for the subdued murmur of their voices, silence reigned and then several rooks lifted out of the branches of the beech trees beside the boundary wall and wheeled above them, calling angrily.

Clay's eyes narrowed and he glanced casually at the guards. None of them took any notice and he turned again to the beech trees, wondering who was hiding there and what they intended.

Sir George took a pace forward and called, 'Well, are you satisfied, Rogan? You've now seen Colonel Fitzgerald and your son for yourself. You know my terms. What have you got to say?'

Shaun Rogan's voice boomed across the ground like an organ. 'Only this, you dog. I'll give you an hour to release the both of them. After that, I'll move against you, and one thing I promise. If you've harmed a hair of their heads, I'll burn Drumore House and you'll roast in its flames.'

Sir George seemed to find difficulty in speaking, so great was his rage. 'By God, you've threatened me for the last time, Rogan,' he cried in a cracked voice.

His hand came of his pocket holding a pistol. As he levelled it, Dennis Rogan gave a cry of warning and, flinging himself down the steps, sent Sir George staggering into Burke and then he ran down the drive toward his father.

Before Clay could move, the guards closed in around him and he stood there helpless to prevent the tragedy that followed. The boy had covered perhaps half the distance to his father, when Sir George calmly took aim, using his left arm as a rest for the barrel, and shot him in the back.

Dennis cried out and seemed to trip, rolling

over several times, and then he struggled to his feet and continued toward the trap, lurching from side to side.

As Sir George took aim again, a bullet kicked gravel from the drive into his face and several horsemen appeared from amongst the beech trees and galloped toward the house, Kevin Rogan leading. Sir George turned and stumbled up into the porch and the guards followed him. Burke came last, backing slowly up the steps, taking deliberate aim and firing until his pistol was empty.

Kevin Rogan dismounted, lifted Dennis from the ground and carried him to the trap. He laid the boy carefully across the seat beside his father, and the old man picked up the reins and, turning the horse in a circle, moved away.

The other four men on horseback kept up a fusillade of shots toward the main door, covering Kevin until he was mounted again. A moment later, he called to them and they all wheeled and galloped through the main gates and disappeared along the road to Drumore.

Clay had flung himself face down on the floor as the shots chased them through the door and now he got to his feet slowly and looked about him. The walls were pitted with bullet holes and a great gilt-framed mirror had splintered into a thousand pieces.

One of the men sat against the far wall, a hand clutching his side, blood welling between his fingers. Clay dropped down to one knee beside him, but as he started to examine him, the man seemed to choke. There was a rattle in his throat, followed by an eruption of blood, and his head lolled to one side.

'He's dead,' Clay announced, getting to his feet.

The guards stirred uneasily and Burke said in a calm voice, 'Hold the colonel there.'

Someone prodded Clay in the ribs with the barrel of a shotgun, as Sir George advanced and examined the body of the dead man. He looked pale, but otherwise perfectly composed. 'It would seem we can expect a little trouble,' he said. 'How many reliable men have we available?'

'There are six of us here, including myself,' Burke told him. 'And the seven you sent down to the village to impose a curfew should be back soon. We could hold the house for a month if necessary, but the cavalry should be here in three or four hours.'

'You're quite right,' Sir George said. 'And we

mustn't forget the servants. Most of them have been in my employ for years.'

'And have loathed and despised you for every moment of that time,' Clay said. 'You bloody murderer. Look around you at the fear on the faces of these men. I wonder how long you'll be able to count on *them* in an emergency.'

Sir George turned toward him, a glazed expression in his eyes. Slowly he wiped spittle from his mouth with the back of one hand and said in a dead voice, 'Take the colonel back to his room, Burke. If he makes the slightest attempt to escape, shoot him.' He disappeared along the passage toward the conservatory as Burke pushed Clay toward the stairs.

As they passed along the landing, a door opened and Joanna appeared, a middle-aged woman in a black bombazine gown at her shoulder, a white mob cap surmounting her vinegary features.

Joanna poised for flight, alarm on her face, and then she recognized Clay and came straight into his arms. 'I heard the shooting,' she said.

The middle-aged woman interrupted in tones of indignation. 'It won't do, Mr Burke. I can't control her. She forced the key from me.'

'That's all right, Mrs Ferguson,' Burke told her.

'You can go.' He turned to Joanna. 'The key, if you please, Miss Hamilton.'

She hesitated and then handed it across, before looking up at Clay anxiously. 'What's been happening?'

Before Clay could reply, Burke took her firmly by one arm and pushed her back into her room, then he closed the door and locked it. Dropping the key into his pocket, he turned to Clay with a sardonic smile. 'And now you, Colonel.'

They moved along the corridor and mounted the stairs to the room on the third floor. Clay sat on the bed and listened to the lock click into place and his heart seemed to turn to stone. What hope was there for him now? What hope at all?

He spent the next hour standing at the window, looking down towards the village, wondering how seriously Dennis Rogan had been wounded. He was the only doctor for miles and his presence could mean the difference between life or death for the lad. He turned away from the window, and the door opened.

Two of Burke's men entered and hustled him out into the corridor. As they pushed him along in front of them, he listened to their conversation. 'I don't like it,' one of them said. 'I don't like it one little bit. There isn't a bloody servant left in the house.'

'Burke knows what he's doing,' the other replied, trying to sound confident. 'We'll be all right.'

They both seemed so nervous and edgy that Clay took heart. They reached the head of the stairs, but instead of going down to the hall, they crossed the landing and turned into another corridor, pausing outside a door. One of the men opened it and the other pushed Clay roughly inside.

Sir George Hamilton lay on a great bed and Burke stood over him, a glass of water in his hand. The agent turned and his face was devoid of expression. 'A chance to exercise your calling, Colonel. Sir George has had some kind of an attack.'

Clay shrugged. 'I've nothing with me, no drugs, no instruments. However, I'll take a look at him if you insist.'

'I do!' Burke assured him. As Clay moved forward, the agent spoke to the two guards. 'Henderson, you join the others down below. You guard this door, Clark.'

The door closed behind them as Clay leaned

over Sir George. His shirt front was stained with foul-smelling blood and his collar had been loosened. As Clay touched him, the eyes opened and Sir George stared up at him, blankly, and then a light seemed to flicker on and his lips moved. 'Take your damned hands off me.'

Clay straightened and turned to Burke. 'There's nothing I can do. Your master is suffering from an incurable disease. He's had these attacks before. Leave him for a couple of hours and he'll be fit to walk again.'

'For how long?' Burke said softly.

Clay shrugged. 'That's impossible to say. I think another such attack will kill him.'

Burke frowned, and then he went and opened the door and called in the guard who stood there. 'Take the colonel back to his room, Clark.'

Clay moved outside and passed along the corridor, Clark at his heels. They walked across the landing and, below, he saw two men lounging by the front door. One of them glanced up and, seeing him, made some ribald comment to his companion.

Clay slowed as he came to Joanna's door and Clark prodded him in the back with the barrel of the shotgun and said roughly, 'Keep moving.'

Clay pivoted neatly, brushing the barrel aside with his wounded arm, and slammed his right fist into the man's exposed neck. Clark staggered against the wall with a groan and slid to the floor.

Clay stood well away from the door and stamped at it with his right foot. After several attempts, the lock gave and the door swung back to reveal Joanna standing on the other side of the room. She ran into his arms.

He held her close for a moment and said gently, 'Are you all right? They haven't harmed you in any way?'

She shook her head. 'There isn't one of them would dare to lay a finger on me. They're too scared of my uncle. But what about you? What was all the shooting about?'

'I haven't got time to explain in detail,' he said, 'but your uncle shot Dennis Rogan in the back.'

'Is he dead?' she said in a shocked voice.

'I don't know,' Clay told her. 'Shaun Rogan carried him away in his trap. I must get to the lad to see if I can do anything. I should imagine all hell is going to break loose round this house within another hour.'

'Then we'd better leave as quickly as possible,'

she said. 'I've got a key to a small door that leads to the stables.'

She led the way, and Clay paused only to pick up Clark's shotgun. The house was filled with an unnatural stillness, a brooding calm, as if everything waited for the storm to break, and he wondered why the servants had left. Presumably word must have come to them from the village, or perhaps the murder of Dennis Rogan and the shooting which followed had been the final straw. One thing was certain, Sir George Hamilton was reaping what he had sown over the long years. Now he was left with only his imported bullies and Burke to protect him until the soldiers arrived, and they would have to be quick.

They descended two flights of servants' stairs and turned into a narrow passageway, at the end of which stood a door. Joanna fumbled with the key for a moment and the door opened.

The cobbled yard was quiet and deserted and the stable doors stood open. Clay peered out cautiously, then he took her hand and started across.

At that moment, a door opened some twenty yards away and Burke came out, two men at his heels. He was obviously unaware that Clark lay unconscious in the passage outside Joanna's room, for he stared at them, astonishment on his face.

In those few seconds of precious time, Clay pushed Joanna through the stable entrance. As he followed, Burke's men fired at him and lead shot scattered through the air. Clay returned the fire, and Burke and his men stepped back into the shelter of the kitchen door to reload.

'Get out while you have the chance, Clay,' Joanna cried, getting to her feet. 'Remember Dennis Rogan needs you. I'll be all right. They won't dare to harm me.'

What she said was right and there was no point in argument. Pegeen was standing in a nearby stall and he led her out and slipped a bridle over her head. He vaulted onto the mare's bare back and smiled down at Joanna.

'I'll be back,' he said savagely. 'I swear it!' He gave a blood-curdling cry and slapped Pegeen on the rump, sending her out through the door.

Burke's men had never heard the Rebel yell before and the sound of it, plus the speed with which Pegeen bolted from the stables, sent them hastily back into the shelter of the kitchen door, as if expecting an attack.

It was Burke who recovered first. Snatching one

of the shotguns, he levelled it and fired. Leaning low over Pegeen's neck, Clay heard the shot whistle through the branches of the trees as he laboured up the slope through the orchard, and then he was through the gap in the wall and safe amongst the trees.

He gave Pegeen her head, gripping her bare sides firmly with his knees, and urged her into a gallop when they reached the moor. Fifteen minutes later, he rode down though the trees to Claremont.

When he went into the kitchen, he found the whole place in complete disorder and there were signs that a struggle had taken place. He went upstairs, two at a time, calling anxiously, but there was no reply. He found his saddlebags lying in a corner where they had been thrown by Burke's men searching the bedroom, and checked that his surgical instruments and drugs were in order as he went back downstairs.

He hurried across to the stables and saw, with a feeling of relief, that the other horse had gone. It was more than likely that Joshua had recovered from his blow on the head and had gone down to the village to see if anything could be done. Clay found a spare saddle and quickly strapped it onto Pegeen's back. A moment later, he galloped down the drive and turned into the main road.

When he entered Drumore, an uncanny silence reigned. An old woman crossed the street hurriedly, pausing only to give him a frightened glance over one shoulder and then a door closed behind her and he heard a bolt rammed firmly into place.

As he drew abreast of Cohan's pub, a familiar voice called to him and Joshua came out of the stable yard, a crude bandage wrapped around his head. 'Am I glad to see you, Colonel.'

Clay grinned down at him. 'It's been a hectic day so far for both of us. How's your head?'

Joshua managed a wry smile. 'It aches some, but I'll survive.'

You'd better fill me in on what's been happening here,' Clay said, dismounting. 'Where is everybody?'

'They've all gone to Drumore House, Colonel,' Joshua said. 'Kevin Rogan called a meeting right here in the centre of the village. He told them how Sir George Hamilton had shot his brother in the back in cold blood.'

'That's true enough,' Clay said. 'I saw it happen. Where is the boy now?'

'He died, Colonel, just after his father brought him into the village in his trap,' Joshua said. 'Mr Rogan's up at the church with him now.'

'But where's Father Costello?' Clay demanded. 'Where was he when all this was going on?'

'There was bad trouble here,' Joshua said. 'Some of Sir George's men arrived and tried to impose a curfew. The mob turned on them, dragged some from their horses. We seemed to be all set for a lynching, when Father Costello arrived. He got three of the men into his house and wouldn't let anybody touch them. The others got away. He's there now.'

Clay considered the situation for a moment, brows knit, and then he swung into the saddle. 'I'm going up to the church to see Shaun Rogan. Wait for me at Father Costello's house.'

He turned Pegeen away, cantered along the muddy street and dismounted outside the tiny church. It was quiet and peaceful as he moved along the path between the ancient, moss-covered gravestones. One of the great oak doors stood slightly open. He removed his hat and stepped inside.

The peace and the quiet of that place enveloped

him, and suddenly he felt very tired, drained of all his strength. The light in the church was very dim, and down by the altar, candles flickered and the image of the Holy Mother seemed to float out of the darkness, bathed in a soft white light.

The smell of the incense was overpowering and he felt giddy and light-headed. He stretched out a hand in the darkness and felt the cold roughness of a pillar in front of him. It brought him back to reality and he walked quietly along the stone-flagged aisle, spurs jingling softly, to where Shaun Rogan knelt in prayer beside the open coffin.

There were no visible signs of violence. They had laid the boy in the coffin still dressed in the clothes he had worn that day, hands crossed on his breast, and his pale face seemed very young.

Clay touched Shaun Rogan gently on the shoulder and the old man looked up at him. He had aged immeasurably since their last meeting. The flesh seemed to hang in folds from his face and his blue eyes were glazed with pain. When he stood up, he sagged at the shoulders, and his feet dragged as they walked away from the altar toward the door.

The sky was darkening and thunder rumbled in the distance. Shaun Rogan carefully placed his hat on his head and said in a dead voice, 'I'm glad you managed to get away from them, Colonel. You'll be needing help to leave the country.'

'I understand Kevin is leading an attack on Drumore House,' Clay said. 'You must use your influence to prevent it taking place. If we hurry, we'll still be in time.'

Shaun Rogan stared at him blankly. 'With one of my sons lying dead in there, murdered in cold blood for the world to see, you want me to stop it?'

'Sir George sent a messenger to Galway this morning,' Clay told him. 'He's asked for the cavalry to turn out. I'm afraid there will be real trouble if we don't persuade the villagers to disperse to their homes.'

Shaun Rogan limped painfully to his trap and climbed into the driving seat. He picked up the reins and shook his head and there was a hard finality in his tone. 'I told you once before that it was dangerous to raise the Devil, Colonel. Today, George Hamilton will find that payment is due. I hope he roasts in hell. Now you must excuse me. My wife is waiting at home for news of our son.'

With a heavy heart, Clay watched him go, the shadow of a man, changed beyond belief, and then he swung into the saddle and galloped back along the street to Father Costello's house.

The priest waited for him on the doorstep and his face was troubled. 'A sad day for Drumore, Colonel. Violence begets violence, as you told me in the inn at Kileen.'

'You knew me, then?' Clay said.

The old priest nodded. 'I know many things, Colonel. A parish priest sees more than people imagine. Have you seen Shaun Rogan?'

Clay shrugged. 'A waste of time, I'm afraid. He refuses to use his influence to disperse the mob. He's gone home to break the news of his son's death to his wife.'

'The people were in an ugly mood when they left here,' Father Costello said. 'I've never seen such anger as was shown when Shaun Rogan arrived with the body of his son. There was nothing I could do to stop them. It took me all my time to save the three poor wretches they dragged from their horses.'

'Where are they now?' Clay said.

'Two of them left here not ten minutes ago. The other had a crack on the head. Your servant is seeing to him inside.'

'That leaves you free to come to Drumore House

with me,' Clay told him. 'Sir George has sent for help to Galway. If the cavalry arrive and find the people attacking the house, they'll cut them to ribbons.'

The priest's face became grave. 'Then I would suggest you ride on ahead and do what you can until I arrive, Colonel. Believe me, you possess greater influence than you are aware, now that the people know of your other identity.'

He turned back into the house and Clay wheeled Pegeen and galloped away along the village street. The sky was now so dark that the light seemed to fail, and he became aware of a strange, sibilant whispering amongst the bare branches of the trees, as a wind seemed to spring up from nowhere. He could hear the sound of the mob when he was still some distance away from the house and then he thundered over the bridge and saw them clustered at the main gates.

The windows of the lodge had been smashed and the door swung crazily on buckled hinges. As Clay rode up, several men ran out of the front door, and an excited murmur rippled through the crowd as a tongue of flame licked at a curtain hanging in a window and blossomed into life. Smoke started to billow through every opening, someone laughed out loud and there was a general, ragged cheer.

One or two of the younger women from the village stood on the edges of the crowd, shawls tightly wrapped about their heads, but the vast majority of those present were men. On the whole, they seemed surprisingly well-armed. Hands gripped rifles convulsively, eyes shone as the flames danced in them. An old man cackled, exposing toothless gums and next to him, a boy shivered with excitement. A dangerous, uneasy frenzy became apparent amongst them and now the voices were no longer separate but one.

When people banded together to stand up for their rights, their integrity of purpose was measured so often only by that of their leaders. It was always the same, he reflected bitterly as he urged his horse toward Kevin, who sat a black stallion by the gate and looked up toward the house.

As people recognized Clay, a cheer broke out and hands reached up to touch him. An expression of astonishment appeared on Kevin's face and he clasped Clay's hand warmly. 'God, but it's good to see ye, Colonel. So you managed to slip those black devils in there?'

'You've got to get out of here,' Clay said urgently.

'You must make these people disperse to their homes. Hamilton sent word to Galway this morning. I've every reason to believe they'll turn out the cavalry.'

Kevin laughed harshly. 'Is it women you think we are, Colonel?' He gestured toward the crowd. 'Look about you. We're well-armed. Twenty of the latest carbines direct from New York, besides fowling pieces and shotguns. This is no rabble of peasants armed with scythes and pitchforks. That lodge is only the beginning. We intend to hang George Hamilton to one of his own trees. If we can't lay hands on him, he can roast inside the house.'

He turned away and gave crisp, incisive orders to one of his lieutenants to take thirty men round to the back. They moved away quickly, skirting the boundary wall and Clay urged Pegeen toward Kevin and said desperately, 'But Joanna is still in there. We must get her out before the shooting starts.'

Kevin shrugged and said in a voice of stone, 'I'm sorry, but it's too late to do anything for her now.'

'Not if I can help it!' Clay said harshly. He forced a way through the crowd, men scattering to avoid

Pegeen's trampling hooves, and then he was clear and galloping up the drive toward the house.

Someone started to fire from a window and he leaned low in the saddle and then the firing stopped. As he dismounted outside the front door, it opened and Burke emerged, the Dragoon Colt in one hand.

'So you've decided to come back to us, Colonel?' he said calmly.

Clay mounted the steps and faced him. 'Dennis Rogan is dead and there's a mob of over a hundred angry people down there who intend to burn you out. I've come for Miss Hamilton. The least you can do is to let her go free before any harm comes to her.'

A strange smile appeared on Burke's face. 'You constantly surprise me, Colonel Fitzgerald. Frankly, I'm beginning to wonder how you ever survived the war.' He cocked the Colt and raised it until it was pointing straight at Clay's heart. 'You'll oblige me by stepping inside.'

The door had been barricaded with furniture, and as they moved in, one of the men closed it and two others pushed a heavy chest of drawers back into place against it.

'That won't hold them for long,' Clay observed.

'It won't need to,' Burke said. 'We expect a little help to arrive soon. When it does, that mob will smile on the other side of its damned face.'

He gestured toward the stairs and Clay moved ahead of him. Burke followed and another guard brought up the rear. They mounted the servants' stairs and halted outside the little room on the third floor in which Clay and Dennis Rogan had been imprisoned that morning. Burke unlocked the door and Clay passed inside.

Joanna was standing at the window and she turned to face them, dismay appearing in her eyes when she saw Clay. He smiled reassuringly and took her hands. 'There's nothing to worry about.'

'I'm afraid you're mistaken, Colonel,' Burke said. 'I haven't the slightest intention of allowing Miss Hamilton to leave, nor do I intend to allow you to slip through my fingers again.' He nodded toward the window. 'You should have an excellent view of the proceedings, but I wouldn't hope for too much if I were you. I'm leaving a guard outside. Please don't try anything foolish.' The door closed behind him.

Clay held Joanna close and frowned slightly. Not for one moment had he imagined that Burke would allow her to leave, but at least they were together again. The point at issue now, was how to get away?

They crossed to the window and stood together, looking out between the bars. The villagers flooded in through the main gate, half a dozen farm carts pushed before them as a shield. Kevin Rogan and several more mounted men rode behind, urging them on with cries.

Somehow it all seemed remote and unreal down there on the grass, like some child's game of make-believe. Then the firing started from the house and the villagers replied. The peculiar acrid odour of burnt powder rose up on the wind and tingled in the nostrils, carrying with it for Clay a hundred memories of battles in the past.

A man screamed and fell forward onto his face, and then another. This was where it started, Clay reflected grimly. The harsh reality and the violence, the pain, the blood.

Joanna gave a tiny moan and her fingers dug into his arm. 'Oh, Clay, it's so futile. So horribly pointless. It won't gain them anything.'

He shook his head and his voice was sombre. 'I'm not so sure. What else is there left for people like these? They accept degradation and brutality for year after year, but finally there comes a time when a man must turn and fight. His final and ultimate protest against any tyrant is to give his life in open defiance, and that can never be futile. One day it will achieve something, one day all the dead and the petty little insurrections over the years will be seen to form part of a pattern. Perhaps then the thing they died for will be achieved.'

'I've never heard you talk like that before,' she said, and looked up at him, a frown on her face.

He laughed grimly. 'Perhaps I've never felt quite like this before. The thing that hurts is the knowledge that soon the military will arrive and that ultimately, whatever happens, these people will be the ones to suffer. Not Burke or your uncle.'

She held his arm and they peered down below as the smoke and the shouting, and the cries of the wounded drifted up toward them and then Clay stiffened. He held his face very close to the bars, and when he turned, his face was grave. 'They've set the house on fire.'

'Are you sure?' she said.

A great dark cloud of smoke billowed up past the window to answer her and Clay ran to the door and hammered on it. 'For God's sake, let us out!' he cried. 'The house is on fire.'

There was a sound of movement outside, and then the guard answered in a frightened voice. 'I haven't got the key – Mr Burke has it.'

'Then go and get it,' Clay insisted.

'But he told me to stay here,' the guard replied, and there was panic in his voice. Suddenly, he gave a stifled exclamation and turned away from the door, and Clay heard him running along the corridor.

12

From below came the sound of breaking glass and then a roar from the mob, and smoke was sucked into the room through the bars, sending a flicker of panic moving inside Clay. Joanna pushed a tendril of hair back from her forehead and said calmly, 'What happens now, Clay? Do you think he'll come back?'

He shook his head. 'Not a chance. From the sound of him, he was scared out of his wits.'

He picked up a heavy wooden chair in both hands and battered it against the door, gritting his teeth against the pain which flooded through his wounded arm. Again and again, he swung the chair, until it splintered in his hands and he dropped it to the floor with a curse.

He looked desperately around the room, but there was nothing – nothing at all, and then Joanna pointed to the bed. 'What about using that? I could help you.'

He pulled the blankets and mattress away and examined the narrow truckle bed. It was solidly constructed of iron, heavy and durable. He tipped it over onto its side and lifted one end. Joanna took the other and, swinging together, they attacked the door.

Almost at once, it started to give and he swung again with renewed vigour, ignoring the pain in his arm. Splinters started to fly, and then a crack appeared in one of the planks as if by magic. The door sagged suddenly in the centre, and although the lock stayed firm, planks bulged outwards under repeated blows. He dropped his end of the bed and tore at the planks with his hands until the gap was large enough to pass through.

Smoke drifted along the corridor toward them and he took Joanna's hand and plunged toward the servants' stairs. They descended to the second floor in safety, but as he put foot on the next flight of stairs, a sudden rush of heat enveloped them and tongues of flame licked at the dry woodwork.

He turned desperately, a great fear in his heart.

From the smell of the smoke, the fire had been started in the lamp oil store and now it was spreading rapidly through the old bones of this ancient house.

He stopped and leaned against the wall, coughing as smoke touched the back of his throat. Joanna leaned against him and she was trembling. She stared back into the past, and for a moment, there was fear and horror in her eyes. He remembered that as a little girl she had lived through just such another hell as this at Lucknow. He held her firmly and said, 'Are you all right?'

Something seemed to flicker in her eyes and she took a deep breath and squared her shoulders. 'Yes, I'm fine. But what are we going to do? The wood in this house is three hundred years old. It will burn like tinder.'

'Is there another staircase?'

She shook her head. 'Only the main one down to the entrance hall.'

A blast of hot air swept along the corridor, moving them on before Clay could consider the position further. What was happening down at the front entrance he had no means of knowing, but it seemed they were going to find out. There was no other choice.

The floor was warm under their feet and smoke rose from the carpeting as it started to smoulder, and then, almost in slow motion, a plank heaved and buckled a few feet in front of them and a tongue of flame flickered through. Clay realized that the whole of the ground floor must be alight, but he held up an arm before his face to ward off the heat and staggered on, pulling Joanna behind him.

Through the crackling of the flames, he could hear the sound of shooting and a confused babble of voices, and then as he descended two steps into a lower reach of the corridor, a figure stumbled out of the smoke and lurched into him.

It was Burke, and a thin trickle of blood oozed sluggishly down one side of his smoke-blackened face from a gash below his left eye. 'There's no way out for you here, you dog,' Clay said, pushing Joanna behind him.

Burke reeled back against the wall and started to raise the Dragoon Colt. Clay kicked the weapon from his grasp, and as it clattered to the floor, kicked it again along the corridor. They came together, breast to breast.

Clay forgot the pain in his arm, forgot everything except his desire to smash this man into the ground. They rolled together upon the floor, hands tearing at each other, and once Clay screamed as flames licked through the floorboards, touching his bare flesh.

And then they were on their feet, Burke a shade faster. As Clay rose, the agent kicked him in the chest, sending him crashing back against the floor. Clay felt as if the very air had been driven from his lungs. He was conscious of something hard pressing against his back, and scrabbled for it as Burke moved forward and raised a boot to stamp down onto his unprotected face. Clay's right hand came out from under him, clutching the Dragoon. He cocked it and fired in the same move at point-blank range.

Burke was pushed back against the wall as the heavy slug tore into his vitals. A strange expression compounded of agony and bitterness appeared on his face, as if he was angry that fate had cheated him to the last. Then blood erupted from his mouth. He folded his hands over his wound, as if to hold in the life which drained from him, sagged slowly at the knees and rolled over on his back.

Clay tried to sit up and Joanna appeared beside him, hair dishevelled, face black with smoke. 'Get up!' she screamed. 'We haven't got a moment to lose.'

He was still holding the Dragoon in his right hand and he thrust it into his pocket and followed her. As they reached the head of the stairs, the smoke cleared. The floorboards of the landing were already on fire and so was the staircase itself. Down below, four of Burke's men still fought desperately behind their barricade, firing out through the side windows.

As Clay pulled out the Colt and started down to the hall, one of the men began to pull away the barricade from the door. 'We'll be burned alive if we stay here any longer,' he screamed.

At the same moment, the stair carpet burst into flames, and Joanna gave a cry of pain and moved down a step hurriedly. The men turned and looked up and Clay raised the Colt. 'Get that door opened before we all roast,' he cried. 'Do as I say and I'll see no one harms you.'

One by one, they dropped their weapons and started to clear the barricade. Clay and Joanna moved to join them, and as the door swung open, Clay shouted, 'Hold your fire! We're coming out!'

Kevin Rogan emerged from behind a farm cart at the bottom of the steps as Clay and Joanna stumbled into the fresh air, the four men following them, hands high.

As Rogan came to meet them, Clay said, 'I persuaded these men to surrender on the understanding that they wouldn't he harmed. I want your promise on that.'

'I'm not interested in these scuts,' Kevin said wildly. 'It's bigger fish I'm after.'

'Burke is dead. I killed him myself,' Clay said.

'And Hamilton?' Kevin demanded. 'Don't tell me he's also dead?'

Clay frowned, realizing that Sir George must still be in his bedroom, and started up the steps back into the entrance hall. As he went through the door, Kevin caught up with him. 'Where is he?' he demanded.

'On the first floor,' Clay told him. 'He collapsed earlier on and Burke had him carried to his room.'

The staircase and the landing were blazing strongly, and as Kevin started toward them, Clay caught him by one arm. 'It's too late,' he cried above the roar of the flames. 'You'll never reach him.'

Kevin turned, teeth bared, and there was madness in his eyes. 'I'll follow him to hell if need be.' He tore himself free and plunged up the stairway.

Clay staggered back as heat reached out to

envelope him and, shielding his eyes with one arm, he looked up at the landing. As Kevin Rogan reached the head of the stairs, Sir George Hamilton appeared from the corridor on the right. His face was white, his eyes dark holes, but there was no fear there. No fear at all.

Kevin gave a cry that could be heard clearly above the crackling of the flames and advanced toward him. When he was a yard or two distant, Sir George raised a pistol in his left hand and shot him through the body. Kevin staggered, clutching at the burning handrail with one hand to steady himself, and then he sprang forward and tore the pistol from the old man's grasp.

One hand fastened about his throat relentlessly, the other gripped his belt. Kevin raised him above his head and tossed him over the balustrade. As he did so, the floor seemed to sag. He clutched at the handrail and the landing dissolved beneath him and he disappeared into a cauldron of flames.

Clay took one hesitant step forward and then the entire ceiling started to collapse. He turned and jumped for the door and staggered out into the fresh air as the hall became an inferno.

He moved down the steps, tearing his smouldering coat from his body, and Joshua pushed through the crowds and took his arm. 'You all right, Colonel?'

Clay nodded, and a hand twisted him round and he looked into the strained white face of Cathal Rogan. 'What happened to Kevin?' he demanded, and there was a tremor in his voice.

Clay tried to speak, but somehow the words refused to come. It didn't really matter, because the thing he wanted to say showed plainly on his face. Cathal Rogan turned blindly away and stumbled toward Marteen, who stood between two horses. Clay watched them speak, saw the younger boy's shoulders sag, and watched as they mounted and rode away through the crowds toward the orchards and the back way up to the moor.

Father Costello sat in his trap, Joanna beside him. She looked sick and faint and there were great rents in her dress where she had torn the smouldering cloth. She opened her eyes and said calmly, 'Is my uncle dead?'

Clay nodded. 'So is Kevin Rogan. A bad day's work.'

'Indeed so, Colonel,' Father Costello said. 'And I fancy it will be a long time before we hear the last of it.' He picked up the reins. 'I'll take Miss Hamilton back to my house for the time being.

What are your own plans, Colonel? I fancy a berth on the first available ship might be advisable.'

Clay nodded soberly. 'I'll have to leave the country as soon as possible. It won't be long before the authorities are on my track. I'll stay here and do what I can to persuade these people to return to their homes. I'll send my servant with you. He may be useful to Miss Hamilton.'

Joshua had been standing at his shoulder and now he climbed into the trap on the other side of Joanna. 'I wouldn't hang around here for too long, Colonel,' he said. 'I've got an idea it's going to become unhealthy.'

'Don't worry,' Clay said. 'I won't take any chances. I'll see you in half an hour.' Father Costello slapped the pony with the reins and it trotted away down the drive and turned through the gates onto the main road.

The crowd fell silent as smoke rose high into the sky and orange flames blossomed from the windows. Now the excitement, now the emotion was passed, Clay saw doubt upon many faces and traces of unease, as if they were just beginning to realise the extent of their act and appreciate the consequences.

Here and there, people slipped away, some

assisting a wounded friend. Clay mounted a farm cart and held up his hand. Faces turned toward him and a strange hush fell upon everyone.

He wiped the sweat from his brow and said in a quiet voice that reached each individual clearly, 'For good or ill, the work here is finished. Sir George sent a messenger to Galway this morning asking for aid from the authorities. You'd best get to your homes before the military arrive.'

Almost at once, the crowd broke, as people turned and started to hurry away. Clay jumped down to the ground and picked up his smouldering jacket. He took out the Colt and checked it. There were still three unused bullets in the drum and he thrust it into his waistband and turned to examine some of the bodies which lay stretched on the grass before the house. As he did so, a troop of cavalry swept in through the main gates and halted.

They moved into line with skill and efficiency, red tunics standing out clearly against the grey stone boundary wall behind them. The mob came to a halt, and there was a silence, and then heavy drops of rain began to spot the ground.

An officer's voice sounded clearly, sabres gleamed, as each man drew with a precision that would have done credit to the parade ground. There was a moment of dreadful stillness, as the whole world seemed to wait, and then a bugle sounded on the evening air and they advanced at the trot.

Most of the crowd scattered, some running back toward the house, others making desperately for the beech trees and the boundary wall, knowing their one chance of safety was to reach the woods.

Clay ran along the front of the house and followed the drive round to the stables. His luck still held. There was no Pegeen, but several saddled horses were tethered to a fence. Obviously, some of the men who had attacked the rear of the house had emptied the stables in case they burned with the rest of the building.

Clay unhitched a black stallion and swung into the saddle. Behind him, hooves thundered and an officer galloped round the corner of the house, sabre ready. He raised it to strike and then an expression of amazement appeared on his face and he lowered his weapon.

It was Vale, the young captain Clay had met at Sir George's reception. Clay urged his mount forward and struck him across his sword arm with the barrel of the Colt. Vale cried out in pain and Clay wrenched the sabre from his grasp and said, 'Sorry, Vale, can't stop to explain now.'

He thrust the Colt back into his waistband and urged the stallion up through the orchard, swinging the sabre in his right hand. A man was running through the trees on his left, scrabbling with his fingers into the soil as he slipped on the wet grass. Behind him thundered a trooper, sabre poised to strike. Clay took the stallion into him sideways. He had one glimpse of the man's startled face beneath the peak of the shako, before he smashed the hilt of his sabre into it, sending him toppling from the saddle.

The fugitive grabbed for the bridle of the riderless horse and Clay, having given him his chance, went on. As he breasted the final slope and moved out of the apple trees toward a gap in the wall, a young lieutenant galloped out of the trees on his left and thundered to meet him.

How many times have I done this? Clay thought. How many times through the long, bitter years, and he swung the sabre with the expertness of the battle-tired veteran and waited grimly. The lieutenant was young, only a boy, with a thin smudge of moustache along his upper lip, and this was all he had ever dreamed of.

At the last, Clay took pity on him. He swayed in the saddle, avoiding the thrust which had been aimed inexpertly at his head, and struck the weapon from the boy's hand. His arm swung in that terrible back cut which knows no guard and lops off limbs as a billhook lops branches. At the last moment, he altered his grip and it was the flat of the blade which thudded across the boy's shoulders, hurling him from the saddle.

Clay flung the sabre away into the rain and took the stallion up through the trees to the moor. The rain was falling heavily now and he galloped along the track to Claremont.

Whatever happened, it was obviously impossible for him to return to the village. There was only one place where he might find safe refuge and that was with the Rogans, but first he needed clothes and money.

As he had expected, there was no sign of life when he rode down into the courtyard at Claremont. It would be some time before Vale and his men came looking for him. He dismounted and ran into the house.

In his spare riding boots at the bottom of the leather travelling truck, he had secreted a hundred gold sovereigns. As he entered the bedroom, he was praying fervently that Burke's men had not discovered them. The boots were still lying in the bottom of the trunk, and as he held up each one in turn, a leather purse fell to the floor.

He pulled on a broadcloth riding coat, the first one which came to hand, found a spare hat and went downstairs quickly. He was beginning to feel light-headed again and he became aware of the deep, burning pain in his left arm. He found a bottle of brandy in the cupboard and took a generous swallow, the liquor burning deep into his stomach.

When he mounted the stallion again, he was feeling a little better, and he took the animal up through the trees and halted on the rim of the moor.

In the distance, a black column of smoke lifted into the rain from Drumore House, but he did not watch it for long. Instead, he looked down at Claremont below him in the valley, and for a moment, sadness moved through him, as he realized that this would probably be the last time he would ever see the place. He turned the stallion away and galloped through the rain toward Hidden Valley.

13

No guard rode out of the beech trees to challenge him as he reached the head of the valley and took the stallion down the steep grassy slope to the farm. They crossed the hollow at the bottom, scrambled up to the track and galloped past the paddock.

The rain fell heavily, a grey curtain that reduced visibility considerably. As he halted outside the house, the door opened and Cathal came out, a carbine in his hands.

A look of intense relief appeared on his face and he lowered the carbine and said, 'God be praised, Colonel. For a moment there when I saw you coming, I wasn't sure who it was. We're all as jumpy as kittens here.'

'You've got good reason to be,' Clay told him

grimly. 'The cavalry arrived just after you and Marteen left. I only got away by the skin of my teeth.'

Cathal nodded soberly. 'We were well started across the moor when we heard the shooting. We guessed what must have happened.' He reached for the bridle and led Clay's horse into the stables. 'Better leave him saddled, Colonel. There's no knowing how fast we may have to get out of here.'

Clay dismounted and led the stallion into a stall next to two other saddled mounts, saw that he was well provided with hay, and followed Cathal across to the house.

The terrible, heartbreaking sound of a woman keening met them in the passage, and Cathal held him back at the kitchen door for a moment. 'That's my mother you hear, Colonel,' he said. 'My father changed his mind about leaving Dennis in Drumore Church and brought the coffin home in the trap.'

'You've told them about Kevin?' Clay asked.

Cathal nodded and there was pain in his young eyes. 'While the one sorrow was upon them, it was best to tell them of the other, Colonel.' He opened the door and led the way in.

The coffin was on the table, a candle burning at

each end in a brass holder. Mrs Rogan sat beside it, a shawl wrapped about her head, and the beads of her rosary clicked between her fingers as she sobbed.

Shaun Rogan sat in his chair by the fire and stared blindly into the flames. The deerhound sprawled at his feet, and as Clay moved forward, its eyes opened and it growled warningly deep in its throat.

Shaun Rogan turned his head and his face was haggard beyond belief, the eyes filmed with moisture. He extended a hand toward an empty chair and said in a dry, unemotional voice, 'Sit ye down, Colonel. It is good to see friends in time of sorrow.'

Cathal produced a bottle of whiskey and two glasses and the old man toasted Clay silently in the ritual drink. Clay emptied his glass. 'There can be little point in my trying to tell you how I feel.'

'I know, you're a friend,' Shaun Rogan answered him. 'You were one of our own from the first. Did my son die well up there at the great house?'

'He took Sir George Hamilton with him,' Clay said.

'And the house itself?'

'Dust and ashes.'

Behind them the woman moaned softly, and Shaun Rogan brooded into the fire. He sighed and it seemed to come from the very depths of his being. 'A poor exchange for two sons, Colonel. A poor exchange. You were right from the first.'

Clay could think of nothing adequate to say in reply, but there was no need. From some inner hardihood of spirit, the old man drew new life. He turned to his two sons. 'We will bury your brother in a little while, decently and with respect, here where he lived. Later, Father Costello can come and bless the ground.'

'We will dig the grave by the bottom wall of the orchard,' Cathal said. 'The ground is soft. It will not take long.'

He gently moved his mother away and Marteen closed the lid of the coffin. They carried it out of the kitchen into the other room and in a little while came the sound of hammer blows as they nailed the lid into place.

Rogan poured himself another drink with a steady hand. 'And what of you, Colonel? Have you any plan for the immediate future?'

'No, but I'll need one,' Clay said. 'The cavalry arrived at Drumore just after the boys left to bring you the news of Kevin's death. I was lucky to get away. It's a known fact that I was Captain Swing, and several of Hamilton's men survived the burning of the house. They'll tell of the part I played. On top of that, I killed Burke.'

Rogan nodded slowly. 'Your trial would be a mere formality, Colonel. A mere formality. 'Tis a good thing you came here and to no other place.'

'You mean you can help me?' Clay said eagerly.

Rogan nodded. 'What you need is a fast boat out of here and that can be provided. There's a French schooner trades into Galway. We have a regular rendezvous with him. It's a common enough thing in Ireland, God help us, for good men to need a quick passage by night.'

'How soon can this be arranged?' Clay asked.

'This very night,' Rogan told him. 'But there's one thing you must do for me in return. Take Cathal and Marteen to America with you. God knows there's little enough for them here in a country that's dying, year by year.'

'I've got a better idea,' Clay said. 'Why don't you come with us?'

The old man smiled sadly. 'The roots are too deep. I'd wither away in any other soil or climate.'

'But what of this rising the Fenians plan for next

year?' Clay said. 'Your sons are members of the Brotherhood. Won't they want to take part?'

'They'll do as I say,' Shaun Rogan said. 'I'll feel happier knowing they're safe in a land where they may prosper by hard work and all men are equal.'

'You think the rising will fail?' Clay said.

'It will fail,' Rogan said heavily. 'As you once told me, England has all the big guns.'

Clay sighed. 'If that's the way you want it, that's the way it will be. I'll take them to California with me. They'll get every chance, I promise you.'

'They'll need money for their passage,' Rogan said.

Clay shook his head. 'I've enough, and to spare, to see us safely to New York. I have ample funds to call on there.'

Shaun Rogan nodded and got to his feet slowly. 'I'll go and tell them about it.' He paused to lay a hand gently on his wife's bowed head and passed out through the door.

Clay listened to the quiet murmur of their voices, and after a while, Marteen came into the room and there was mud on his boots. He helped his mother gently to her feet and said quietly, 'If you could give us your assistance, I'd be grateful, Colonel.'

Clay followed them out into the passage. He gave his arm to Mrs Rogan, who leaned heavily against him, and Cathal and Marteen picked up the coffin and moved through the back door after their father.

They crossed the yard and entered an old walled orchard and the rain fell heavily into the long grass and dripped from the bare branches of the trees.

They had hastily dug the grave in a flower bed against the ivy-covered wall and Shaun Rogan moved forward to inspect it. 'It's only four feet deep, Father,' Cathal told him in a low voice. 'We hadn't time to do any better.'

His father nodded. 'He will rest easy enough here and no one to disturb him.'

Marteen was carrying two lengths of rope and they quickly improvised slings and lowered the coffin into the grave. Afterwards, they stood for a while, heads bowed while their father prayed.

Clay was to remember that moment for long afterwards. The rain, cold and bitter as death as it soaked into his shoulders, a spider's web across an open gate in the wall, a broken sickle half-buried by leaves at his feet. Shaun Rogan's voice moved on and stopped. He picked up a handful of earth and tossed it down onto the coffin, and then he turned and led his wife away through the rain back to the house.

Clay waited until the boys had filled in the grave and they all returned together, Cathal and Marteen discussing plans in a low voice. The French schooner would be half a mile offshore at nine o'clock and stay for two hours. A lantern flashed four times from the beach was the signal that would bring in a longboat.

The boys stayed by the back door to clean the mud from their boots, and Clay went inside. Shaun Rogan sat by the fire alone, a glass in his hand. 'You'll excuse my wife, Colonel. She's gone to lie down.'

Clay sat on the edge of the table. 'There's one thing bothering me,' he said. 'My servant is in Drumore with Miss Hamilton. Father Costello is sheltering her for the moment. I'm wondering if I could get in to see them.'

The old man shook his head. 'Drumore will be crawling with soldiers. You'd be putting your head into a noose if you tried.'

'A message then?' Clay said.

'Who's to take it?' Shaun asked, and shook his head. 'No one but a fool would venture abroad this day. Each man will sit by his fireside and pretend he knows nothing of what happened at Drumore House.' He leaned forward. 'Never worry, man. I'll let the girl know later what happened to you. If she truly loves you, she'll follow you to the world's end.'

Clay nodded slowly. 'Perhaps you're right. At least she's got Joshua with her. He'll look after her.'

'Of course I'm right,' Shaun Rogan said. 'You're no good to her dead, are you?'

Marteen and Cathal entered the room and moved to their father's side. They were dressed for travelling, in tweed riding coats, and carried their hats in their hands.

Shaun Rogan looked up at them and said calmly, 'You'd best not bother your mother. She's stood enough for one day.' Marteen was near to tears and the old man scowled and gripped him by the arm. 'If ye bawl before the colonel, I'll never forgive you.' He smiled and held out his hand. 'Now off ye go, like good lads. Don't disgrace the name, and write to us now and then.'

They shook hands, and as they hurried from the room, Marteen was struggling to hold back his sobs. Shaun Rogan got to his feet, and when he faced Clay there were tears in his eyes. He held out his hand. 'Look after them for me, Colonel.'

For one long moment, Clay clasped hands and stared into those great, calm eyes. 'We ran a good course together, Shaun Rogan,' he said.

A hint of a smile touched the old man's mouth. 'That we did, Colonel. That we did.'

He sagged back into his chair and Clay hurried out of the room and through the passage. As he emerged on the front steps, the boys led the horses from the stables. They mounted, and Clay said, 'Where do we go from here?'

'A place we know of in the hills, Colonel,' Cathal told him. 'We'll be safe there until it's time to leave. The soldiers are bound to call at the farm.'

'And your father?' Clay said.

Cathal shrugged. 'They can't blame him for what his sons do.'

They took the track up to the head of the valley and rode across the moors, and gradually the rain slackened and then stopped. In the distance they could still see smoke rising from the ruins of Drumore House, and as they reached a fork in the path, Cathal reined in and shielded his eyes. 'Who would have thought the place could have burned so.'

Marteen turned to Clay. 'What happened to that servant of yours, Colonel, and Miss Hamilton?'

Clay shook his head. 'I'm not sure. I sent them down to Drumore with Father Costello.'

Marteen frowned. 'Perhaps they've gone to Claremont, hoping to find you there?'

It was a thought which had already occurred to Clay, and now he looked across the moor at the trees a quarter of a mile away, lining the valley in which lay Claremont. He came to a sudden decision. 'I'm going to ride over to find out. You two can stay here. I'll only be twenty minutes.'

Cathal grabbed hold of his bridle. 'It's madness, Colonel. The soldiers are bound to be there.'

'I'll be careful,' Clay assured him. 'I'll stay in the trees and check before going down.'

He cut short further argument by spurring his horse away, but before he had gone far, hooves thundered across the turf behind him and Cathal and Marteen rode alongside.

'There's no need for this,' Clay said.

Cathal shrugged. 'You're our ticket to America, Colonel. We can't afford to lose you.'

They slowed to enter the wood, Clay leading. Out of some strange sixth sense he had a sudden premonition of the danger that waited for them. There was a movement in the trees, a flash of scarlet. He reined in sharply and a voice called, 'Halt in the Queen's name.'

A trooper appeared from the trees, cutting across his path. Clay ducked under the sabre and dashed his fist into the man's face, sending him reeling from the saddle. The stallion plunged on, trampling the fallen man. Suddenly Clay was surrounded by troopers. He drew his Colt and slashed sideways with the barrel, forcing his way through the confused melee of horses and riders.

Then he was through and a voice called to him. He took the stallion up through the trees to where Cathal waved him on, and as he topped the rise he saw, with a thankful heart, that Marteen was already well out in front, galloping strongly for the safety of the hills.

Behind them, a bugle sounded. Clay glanced back over his shoulder and saw a half-troop of cavalry emerge from the woods and gallop after them, spreading out into a fan shape. He thought it a strange proceeding, but as he turned his head, he saw the other half of the troop crossing the moor on their left to cut them off.

He leaned low over the neck of the stallion and

spurred it. The beast responded gallantly. Slowly, he drew nearer to Cathal and then he was at his tail. Another desperate burst of speed and they had passed, with twenty yards to spare, the riders who had tried to cut them off.

The hills lifted to meet them and the horses started to labour. They splashed across a marsh and entered a narrow valley. At the end of it, Marteen dismounted and, holding the reins in his right hand, struggled up the steeply sloping side of the valley, pulling the horse behind him.

He reached the top safely and turned to give his brother a hand. Clay was a yard or two behind them, when several riders appeared in the valley below. Clay slapped the stallion on the rump, sending it up and over the rim of the valley, and then he turned, drawing the Dragoon Colt from his waistband.

There had been enough bloodshed that day. Enough and to spare. As the first trooper reined in his horse, Clay took careful aim and shot the animal through the chest. It reared up, throwing its rider into the mud, and behind him, the rest of the troop fought to turn away their mounts from what appeared to be a death trap. He sent one more bullet singing into the air above their heads, then mounted the stallion which Cathal was holding for him and they galloped away.

They were safe enough after that. Marteen led the way, twisting and weaving from one valley to another, splashing through marsh and bog, all the time working steadily higher into the hills. They rode for an hour in single file before emerging from a small valley onto a steep hillside.

Before them, no more than two miles away, lay the sea, and below, a small loch cut deep into the heart of the hills, black with depth near the centre, purple and grey near the edges where basalt ledges lifted to the surface. Clay dismounted and stood in the desolate light of gloaming, looking north to where the peaks of the mountains were streaked with orange.

The beauty of it was too much for a man, and he breathed deeply on the sweetness of the heather, still wet after heavy rain, then followed Cathal and Marteen down the steep hillside, past a trickle of water that fell through drooping ferns. They reached a rough track, mounted again and rode along the side of a loch, following a running stream which gurgled through the quiet evening.

Behind them the hills lifted in a smooth swell into the dark arch of the sky, where already a single star shone, and as they turned a curve in the valley, he saw a small hunting bothy in a green loop of grass beside the river.

It was stoutly built of dressed stone and roofed with turf. As Marteen dismounted, he said, 'We'll be safe enough here, Colonel. It's only half an hour to the cliffs. The tide will be out and we can follow the beach to the place where the Frenchman is landing.'

He and Cathal sprawled on a crude bench and talked of America in subdued tones. With the natural resilience of youth, the past was already becoming of less importance to them than the future. Clay walked away and sat on a boulder by the river.

His wounded arm nagged at him constantly and his mouth was dry as a bone. He leaned down and scooped water up in the palm of his hand, savouring the coldness of it with conscious pleasure.

He thought of Joanna and was filled with a feeling of savage loneliness and his heart seemed to dry and wither inside him. Whatever a man tried to do, Fate always dealt the last card – that was life. By accepting it, a man saved himself a great deal of pain.

For a moment, he was filled with that terrible

knowledge of his own littleness that comes to a man from time to time. He had known it before, standing amidst the carnage of the battlefield, realizing that next time it could be him, accepting that whatever one did always led nowhere.

Above his head, a single cloud of red fire seemed to burn itself out as he watched, and then the light died on the bald faces of the hills, and night dropped its heavy cloak across the valley.

He sat there for a long time, gazing out toward the sea blindly. Finally, Cathal came and tapped him on the shoulder. They mounted and rode away from that place, their harness jingling softly in the night.

They went carefully, keeping to the shadows of the valley, dismounting when they reached the cliffs, to lead their horses down a treacherous, crumbling track, with boulders gleaming whitely in the moonlight below.

The sand stretched before them, wet and shining in the moonlight where the sea had receded. Cathal spurred his mount into a gallop and they thundered along at the water's edge, occasionally riding belly-deep through the sea to round a spur of rock into another bay.

The ship lay half a mile offshore, her spars and

rigging etched clearly against the night sky. Clay looked up at the moon with a slight feeling of panic, wishing for a cloud to dim its light until they were safely on board.

Marteen laughed excitedly and rode out into the breakers to round another point of rock. Cathal followed him and Clay brought up the rear. A wave sucked them out, and as the stallion began to swim, water slopped over Clay's knees and the cold chill of it somehow brought him back to life, so that he laughed as excitedly as Marteen had done.

And then they were splashing onto the beach and the longboat waited a hundred yards away, floating in shallow water, four seamen at the oars while another stood knee-deep in the water.

'We're in luck,' Cathal shouted over his shoulder. 'No need for a lantern tonight.'

The boys dismounted quickly, and Marteen ran forward into the sea and clapped the seaman on the shoulder. 'Three passengers, me bucko.'

The man said something unintelligible in reply, and as Clay approached, Marteen explained with a smile, 'He only speaks French, Colonel.'

Clay turned to the seaman and said in perfect French, 'We desire a quick passage out of here, my friend. I'm told you can arrange this?'

The sailor beamed. 'Colonel Fitzgerald?' Clay nodded and the man continued. 'We have been waiting for you. Please get into the boat as quickly as possible.'

'You were expecting us?' Clay said in astonishment as they clambered over the gunwale.

'But naturally, Monsieur,' the seaman replied, taking the helm.

Clay sat in the prow and looked back toward the beach as the oarsmen pulled strongly for the ship. The three horses stood at the water's edge, looking rather forlorn, and he thought with a pang of Pegeen and wondered who her new owner would be. Then the stallion lifted his head and snorted and the horses turned and galloped away along the beach in the moonlight.

As the longboat approached the schooner, the anchor was already being raised and sails unfurled. Sharp commands in French drifted clearly across the water, and then they were bumping against the side.

Marteen and Cathal mounted the rope ladder first, Clay following. As he stepped over the rail, a tall, angular man in reefer jacket and salt-stained cap moved forward and held out his hand. 'Colonel Fitzgerald?' he said in English. 'I am Captain

Jourdain. I hope we can make you comfortable until we reach Bordeaux. If you go below now, you will find someone waiting to show you to your cabin. For the moment, you must excuse me. I shall not feel happy until we are well away from here.'

He moved along the deck to the wheel, giving orders in a low voice, and Cathal scratched his head in puzzlement. 'Now wouldn't you say they were expecting us, Colonel?'

Clay nodded, frowning. 'It certainly looks that way.' He shrugged. 'Your father must have got word to them somehow.'

'What are you worrying your head about?' Marteen asked his brother. 'Let's go below and see what kind of a cabin they've given us. I've heard queer things about these French boats.'

They went down the companionway, talking excitedly together, and Clay walked toward the prow and stood, one hand on a shroud, and looked back toward Ireland.

'Are you sorry to be leaving?' a quiet voice said.

For a moment, he remained motionless, and then he turned slowly. She was standing by the mast, a dark cloak about her, and Joshua was at her shoulder. Joshua smiled and turned away along the deck as Joanna moved closer.

Clay pulled her into his arms, kissing her, and then pushed her away and shook his head in bewilderment. 'But how? I don't understand.'

'Father Costello,' she said simply. 'He knew about this boat, although he wasn't supposed to. He knew it would be your only way out of the country.'

'But how did you get out of Drumore?'

She shrugged. 'Father Costello is a very resourceful man. We lay in the bottom of the trap and he covered us with a rug. Captain Vale gave him a special pass to visit the bereaved at some of the outlying farms.'

'Did you see Vale yourself?'

She nodded. 'Yes, he made it his business to find me straight away.'

'Did he have anything to say about me?'

'Only that he didn't understand you.'

Clay laughed lightly. 'That's hardly surprising. I don't even understand myself.' He sighed and there was great bitterness on his face. 'I wonder if it will ever change, if there is any hope for those people back there?'

'There is always hope,' she said firmly. 'God lets no man suffer for too long.'

'Fate plays strange tricks at times,' he said. 'I

arrived in Ireland looking for peace and quiet. Instead I found a situation I couldn't ignore. Now I'm leaving, a hunted fugitive, lucky to escape a hanging.'

'You consider your visit an entire misfortune, then?' she said, gazing up at him and the moonlight glinted amber and gold in her dark eyes.

He gazed back. 'Not an entire misfortune,' he said. 'No.'

He cupped her face in his hands and gently kissed her on the mouth. His arm slid around her waist and she leaned against him. He gave her no other answer, for it was not needed. Together, they looked their last on Ireland, as it merged into the dark horizon of night.